"This is a big deal, Waylon. I'm the ADA. You're a detective. I can't be shacked up with you."

"We're not shacking up. It's protective custody." His grip tightened on the steering wheel. "You're used to controlling everything and all situations. But this is something you can't control. As a prosecutor, you rely on the expertise of others on a regular basis. Use mine now. Don't think of me as your ex. Only as a professional who also happens to be your friend. Let me keep you safe, and stop fighting me. Can you do that until we figure out what's going on and put a stop to it?"

She was fighting their chemistry, his raw sexual magnetism, her attraction to him that was still as strong as ever and her desire for something with him that she couldn't have more than she was fighting him.

Not that he would appreciate the distinction.

Her whole career, she had never been anything but careful. Until she got involved with Waylon Wright.

WYOMING DOUBLE JEOPARDY

JUNO RUSHDAN

Harlequin

INTRIGUE

For Gloria

Recycling programs for this product may not exist in your area.

ISBN-13: 978-1-335-45729-5

Wyoming Double Jeopardy

Copyright © 2025 by Juno Rushdan

Harlequin Enterprises ULC
22 Adelaide St. West, 41st Floor
Toronto, Ontario M5H 4E3, Canada
www.Harlequin.com

Printed in U.S.A.

Juno Rushdan is a veteran US Air Force intelligence officer and award-winning author. Her books are action-packed and fast-paced. Critics from *Kirkus Reviews* and *Library Journal* have called her work "heart-pounding James Bond–ian adventure" that "will captivate lovers of romantic thrillers." For a free book, visit her website: www.junorushdan.com.

Books by Juno Rushdan

Harlequin Intrigue

Cowboy State Lawmen: Duty and Honor

Wyoming Mountain Investigation
Wyoming Ranch Justice
Wyoming Undercover Escape
Wyoming Christmas Conspiracy
Wyoming Double Jeopardy

Cowboy State Lawmen

Wyoming Winter Rescue
Wyoming Christmas Stalker
Wyoming Mountain Hostage
Wyoming Mountain Murder
Wyoming Cowboy Undercover
Wyoming Mountain Cold Case

Fugitive Heroes: Topaz Unit

Rogue Christmas Operation
Alaskan Christmas Escape
Disavowed in Wyoming
An Operative's Last Stand

Visit the Author Profile page at Harlequin.com.

CAST OF CHARACTERS

Waylon Wright—A former army ranger turned cop. He won't let anything, or anyone, stop him from protecting the woman he loves. Not even a killer who is always two steps ahead of him.

Melanie Merritt—The strong-willed, tough assistant district attorney is determined to achieve her professional goals, even if it means sacrificing love. Her whole career, she has never been anything but careful. Until the night Waylon Wright walked into her life.

Holden Powell—This part-time rancher and full-time sheriff's chief deputy owes Waylon and is willing to do him a favor.

Javier Jimenez—Denver PD detective and Melanie's friend.

Brent Becker—No one is more narcissistic than this Denver district attorney who is more concerned about his career than Melanie's safety.

Isaac Meacham—The charismatic cult leader of the Sand Angelites and self-proclaimed pacifist. But what is he hiding, and how far is he willing to go to protect his secrets?

Erica Egan—This journalist will cross any line for a scoop and to see her name in the byline.

Chapter One

It was another typical Thursday evening until it wasn't. A fourteen-hour workday. Always the first one in. Always the last one out.

Gathering her things, she grabbed the fragrant bundle of flowers from a chair and then closed the door to her office. She glanced at the plaque on the door, engraved Assistant District Attorney, Melanie Indira Merritt.

"One day it won't be assistant," she muttered to herself. Her time would come.

Melanie had put in tremendous effort and had the keenest talent when it came to picking a jury, leading to her pristine victory record and earning her the nickname of *The Closer*.

Her previous boss had had a bad habit of taking credit for her work, but things were different at her position here in Laramie, Wyoming. This DA didn't use her and didn't try to sleep with her. More of a father figure, Gordon championed her successes, invited her into his home for meals with his wife, and helped make her transition to the Cowboy State a smooth one.

She walked down the hall of the third floor of the county courthouse where the prosecuting attorney's offices took up the entire space and locked the inner door. Her stomach grumbled, reminding her she'd missed dinner.

Adjusting the straps of her laptop case and purse on her shoulder, she glanced at her watch: 9:10 p.m. Too late for anything heavy. A Caesar salad waited for her in the fridge.

She pushed through the outer door into the attached covered parking garage. The muggy July wind had died down and cooled off. A light rain had started. In the Wyoming valley, where Laramie and Bison Ridge sat, surrounded by the mountains, the temperature in the summer evenings was often mild and pleasant, which beat a blustery winter breeze slicing through her.

She watched Darcy Rosenfeld pull out of her parking spot. The paralegal was great at helping her prepare for meetings and trials. The young woman was thorough, saving Melanie tons of time.

At the trash receptacle, Melanie stopped and took one last whiff of the bouquet of flowers cradled in her arm. Roses, freesia, sweet pea, peonies and hyacinth. Her favorites. They smelled divine, rich in summer colors that would brighten anyone's day.

She read the card once more.

To M&M—no nuts,
This sucks. I hate it. I miss you. Miss the us that might've been. Please rethink this. Soon. Can't wait forever.
Your Cowboy.

Melanie bit back a sad smile. Waylon was holding on to false hope that she would backtrack, go against common sense and a healthy instinct for professional self-preservation. At least he'd stopped calling, leaving enticing voicemail messages that tempted her willpower.

He needed to move on. They both did. But she was far too busy to find someone more suitable, who wasn't a threat to her career.

She tossed the gorgeous bouquet into the trash bin.

Darcy pulled up and rolled down her passenger's-side window. "I'd kill for Hank to buy me a bouquet like that," she said, referring to her boyfriend, a sweet paralegal at a local firm. "Maybe I'll drop a hint. Hey, even if the relationship is kaput, you should keep the flowers. Must've cost a fortune. Sure you don't want to tell me who the cowboy is? It'll be our secret."

Sharing was how secrets ceased to exist. "Good night, Darcy. See you tomorrow."

"Your cowboy, whoever he is, has excellent taste. Not only in flowers." The grinning paralegal waved bye and drove off.

Waylon was definitely unlike any man Melanie had been with. A salt-of-the-earth straight shooter. Humble. Handsome despite his scars or perhaps because of them. Emotionally available.

A great lover.

And a crackerjack detective with the Laramie Police Department, constantly arresting dangerous criminals she had to prosecute.

Therein lay the complicated problem.

When it came to choosing the right guy, she was a horrible failure.

Loneliness crowded in on her, making her ache for something she couldn't have. Not with Waylon. She reached into the trash bin and took out the flowers, against her better judgment. They'd die in a week on their own. No need for her to hurry their demise. Besides, Darcy was right. Waylon had paid a pretty penny for the huge bouquet. She'd never chuck a hundred dollar bill out the window because the wrong person had given it to her.

A yawn took hold. She needed to get home, eat and rest. So, she could rise and shine at the crack of dawn, go for a run, and do it all over again.

Yay, me.

Pulling her car keys from her purse, Melanie headed for her SUV, the lone vehicle remaining on the top level, tucked beside a concrete pillar. Her keys jangled in her hand and her high heels click-clacked across the pavement, echoing in the garage. Raindrops pitter-pattered on the roof of the building and asphalt on the street. She liked to park midway in the lot. Far enough to get in some extra steps on her pedometer. But not too far to make her uncomfortable at night in the public parking garage alone.

These past six months without Waylon, she was always alone.

Maybe time to get a pet. A fluffy, warm independent cat to cuddle. Too bad she was allergic.

She pressed the button on her fob—the horn beeped and the lights flashed—unlocking the SUV, and dropped the keys in her suit pocket.

Footsteps shuffled somewhere behind her. The nape of her neck prickled as she wheeled around toward the sound.

No one. Not a soul in sight.

She listened.

Silence, other than the rain.

She scanned the nearly empty upper floor, searching for anyone lurking, any sinister shadows in dark corners, but she didn't see anything of concern. Nothing out of the ordinary.

Was her mind playing tricks on her? Served her right for working herself to the bone every day.

Dismissing it as fatigue, she started for her SUV. She walked with care, trying to lessen the clatter of her heels.

More footsteps—the sound whispering beneath the noise of her shoes.

Unease slid down her spine. She stopped and surveyed her surroundings again with even more vigilance.

This was a small town, where everyone knew everyone. None of the dangers of a big city, like random muggings, drug addicts driven to desperation. Crime still existed. Usually of a higher order.

Looking around, she didn't see anyone.

The lot was well lit, the street below quiet. The sheriff's office was in the same building on the first floor, and she was well acquainted with everyone in the department. An attendant was in the booth on the main level until ten. She was fine.

Perfectly safe.

Still…

Tension gnawed at the base of her spine.

Trust your instincts. That's what her parents and self-defense classes had taught her.

She tightened her grip on the leather straps of her bags. Digging in her purse for her cell phone just in case, she quickened her pace to her SUV. Her pulse picked up. Sweat trickled in a cold line down her back. Almost there.

Almost.

Movement out of the corner of her eye snatched her attention. She whirled back around.

A man lunged from behind a concrete pillar and rushed toward her. Dressed in dark clothing. Wearing a full-face helmet. Dark-tinted visor. Something long and metallic in his hand.

A crowbar!

Her heart seized. She stumbled backward.

He plowed into her, shoving her up against her vehicle. The flowers tumbled from her arm. He raised the steel bar and swung. She ducked, narrowly missing the blow intended for her skull that crashed against the roof instead.

Melanie punched his stomach and rammed her knee up into his groin. With a grunt, he doubled over and staggered away. She jerked sideways and ran. But he snatched the back of her suit jacket, stopping her.

"Help! Help me!"

Grabbing the laptop case's strap, she swung the bag, using it as an improvised weapon. She slammed it down against his arm, freeing herself of his grip. But her purse slipped off and fell. Another swing with all her strength knocked the crowbar from his other hand and it clattered to the concrete floor. She kicked the steel bar, sending it skittering under the SUV. Then she slung the laptop case up at his head.

He lurched back, his arms flailing.

She dropped the bag and took off running, cursing her stupid heels and the tightness of her skirt. Taking the ramp would lead to the attendant's booth and the sheriff's office. But her assailant was faster and stronger. He could easily overtake her on the way down two stories. Same problem with the stairs.

Keys jangled in her pocket. Avoiding the ramp and staircase, she bolted back toward the building.

Footsteps thundered after her. Melanie flung the exterior door open and ducked inside. She dared to look back. Through the glass panel, she spotted him. He was up and running straight for her.

She raced for the interior door to the office space and snatched the keys from her pocket.

Faster, faster! Run faster!

The keys slipped from her fingers, hitting the carpet. She dashed back and grabbed them. With shaking hands, she fumbled for the right one.

Hinges squeaked behind her. She cast a terrified glance over her shoulder. He stormed through the outer door leading from the garage. She shoved the key into the dead bolt and unlocked the frameless glass door.

He was closing in, charging toward her like an angry bull. *Oh, God!*

She pulled the key free, darted inside and flipped the latch on the dead bolt just as he raced up to the door. Now there was a locked barrier between them.

He yanked on the handle, making the glass vibrate.

What did he *want*?

Unable to get inside, he slapped the door. She backed away,

watching him. He tilted his head to the side and studied the door from top to bottom.

The eerie movement sent a chill over her skin.

Then he smashed his head against the door. Once. Twice. Under the force of the helmet, the glass splintered.

Melanie's heart clenched. She had to get to a phone. Call for help. Once the sheriff's department got the message, a deputy could get to her in less than two minutes.

Unless that man reached her first.

The cracked webbing of the door spread. Panic zipped through her veins hot as an electric current, driving her to move.

Melanie spun around and ran. Not to her office. If he knew who she was, and this wasn't some random attack, then he'd expect her to head there.

But where to go? None of the office doors locked.

Her pulse skittered. Her legs shook. Her mind raced even as time slowed to a crawl.

The glass shattered. He was coming. He was behind her, erasing the distance between them at a frightening rate.

She darted to the left, down a walkway. Her heel caught on the carpet. She tripped and fell hard, scraping her bare leg. Climbing to her feet, a shoe came off. She surged forward, leaving the heel behind, and scanned the open cubicles where legal assistants, witness advocates and interns worked. With only half walls dividing the section, hiding there, virtually out in the open, wasn't a possibility.

No time to hide. She had to call 9-1-1. Reaching over the half wall, she grabbed the receiver. Stabbed the number nine.

The next thing she knew he was on her.

Strong hands flung her against the back wall and clamped around her throat. Melanie struggled and bucked to break free. Tried to throw another knee in that tender spot that would hurt him most.

But he turned at an angle, wedging one of his legs between her thighs. The stench of tobacco registered in her brain. She punched his forearms, hitting solid muscle, not making his grip budge in the least. Ice formed in her chest. She fought to get him off her. Every cell in her body strained with effort.

He had her, his hands locked in a viselike grip around her neck. She tried to scream. No air. Her lungs burned.

Fingers dug into her skin, pressing down on her windpipe, filling her with bone-deep fear. It felt as though her heart was being squeezed in a fist. He slammed her head into the wall. The stunning blow shook her hands loose from his arms. He did it again.

Pain exploded in the back of her skull, blurring her vision. Tears stung her eyes. Much more of that and he'd knock her unconscious.

Melanie prayed he wasn't wearing steel-toed boots and thrust her remaining heel down onto his foot. He flinched.

His feet were vulnerable.

She stabbed the pointed heel down again with far more force. His hands loosened and he reared back a step. She kicked his shin, aiming the heel at bone and then launched her foot into his groin.

Turning, she fled. But she didn't make it far.

He pounced, tackling her to the floor. They wrestled, each struggling to gain the advantage. She threw an elbow into his throat.

Melanie scrambled up from the floor. And so did her attacker.

He grabbed her and threw her into the wall. His gloved hands seized her throat again. He maneuvered his lower half, pressing his knees between hers, protecting himself. His grip on her tightened, shutting off her airway.

A scream was strangled and died in her throat. She wanted to ram the heel of her palm up into his nose to break it the way she'd been taught in self-defense class, but the helmet protected his face.

His face.

If she could see him, identify him, scratch him, claw his eyes, get his DNA under her nails in the event of a worst-case scenario in which she didn't make it out of this alive, that would be something.

A fierce sense of determination rushed through her veins. No matter what, she was going to take this guy down. Regardless of the personal cost.

Melanie resisted the instinct to pry his hands from her throat and reached for the visor. She shoved it, but the face shield didn't move. Like it had been glued shut.

One of his hands released the pressure against her windpipe. She sucked in a ragged breath.

A fist blasted into her jaw, knocking the air from her lungs. She reeled from the blow, but if he didn't like her messing with his face shield, then she had to get it up.

She scraped and clawed at the visor, prying her nails into the seam. Breaking several gel tips down to the nail bed, she forced a sliver of the dark-tinted shield up. He slammed another fist into her.

Agony left her dazed, struggling to stay on her feet.

Letting her go, the man spun away, lowering his head and adjusting the visor while she pressed herself against the wall, hauled in desperate breaths through the gut-wrenching pain and felt around for something, anything, to help her get out of this nightmare.

Her fingers grazed cold metal.

A fire extinguisher.

She unhooked it from the wall and swung the extinguisher like a baseball bat, smashing it into his head. He spun, thrown off balance. Not giving him a chance to recover, she rammed the butt of the extinguisher into his gut. She hit him again and again, this time over the back of the head, wanting to crack the helmet open.

He dropped to his knees and pitched forward, putting a hand to the floor to steady himself. She pulled the pin on the fire extinguisher, breaking the tamper seal, pointed the nozzle at him and squeezed the handle, spraying him with the extinguishing agent.

The man coughed and grunted.

Melanie spun on her heel and ran to the district attorney's office at the far end of the hall. She slammed the door shut behind her. Dropped the extinguisher. Grabbed a chair. Jammed the sturdy back under the lever door handle.

The next best thing to a lock.

But was it enough?

She hurried to the desk. Shoved it across the room with items on the top clattering to the floor. Pushed it against the door as a barricade.

Dread clogged her throat. She wiped moisture from her nose with the back of her trembling hand. Her face throbbed where he'd hit her and her heart hammered against her ribs. She picked up the extinguisher and clutched it to her chest. Something inside her needed to keep the makeshift weapon close.

She searched the floor and saw the landline phone.

On quivering legs, she stumbled to it, dropped to the floor in a shaking, terrified puddle and picked up the receiver.

Blood was on her hands, on the phone. Her blood.

Pressing her back to the desk, digging the heels of her feet into the carpet, pushing against it with all her weight to prevent him from getting inside the room, she dialed for help.

"This is 9-1-1, what's your emergency?"

Chapter Two

Detective Waylon Wright cut his gaze from the deputy assigned to do forensics work near Melanie's car and eyed the bouquet he'd sent her that had been trampled to pieces. He stalked toward the building, ducked under the crime scene tape and headed down the short walkway.

At the shattered door, he stepped on broken glass, the shards crunching under his boots.

Entering the offices of the district attorney, he wiped any trace of the feelings roiling through him from his face and walked down the hall. He was about to make a right toward Melanie's office but noticed the gaggle of deputies at the other end of the floor.

On his way there, a spot in the hall caught his attention and he stopped. There were signs of a struggle and remnants of fire-extinguishing agent. He looked around before he made his way to the DA's office. Deputies Cody and Lee blocked the threshold with their backs to the hall. Waylon put a hand on Lee's shoulder. The guy glanced at him and stepped aside, letting him through.

The office was in shambles. Melanie sat in a chair. An ice pack pressed to her cheek. An EMT examining her. Mel's nose was bloody. The usual slick twist she wore was loose and messy, with wild black strands hanging around her face. She spoke in a firm, steady voice, giving a statement to chief deputy Holden Powell, who was crouched in front of her.

Waylon's mood darkened as he listened. Rage filled him, his fingers curling into fists. But relief seeped through, too. She was alive.

"Once I managed to get away from him, I called 9-1-1." Mel's gaze flashed up to his. A flicker of unguarded emotion crossed her face, horror suddenly alive in the depths of her brown eyes. Tears glistened and one rolled down her cheek.

Looking away from him, she lowered her head and whisked the moisture from her eyes.

Holden glanced over at him and stood. "Waylon. What's the LPD doing here?"

"I was getting ready to head home, heard about the attack on the radio, and the APB for the suspect." Not that the all-points bulletin had provided much to go on. Male. Dressed in all black. Wearing a dark-tinted motorcycle helmet. Approximately six feet tall. Medium build. "Figured I'd swing by. Take a look around. Unofficially, of course. Make sure the town's favorite ADA is okay."

"Hope you're not planning to try and steal this case." Holden put his hands on his hips.

Melanie straightened. "I don't want him working on this one. He shouldn't even be here."

Gritting his teeth, Waylon gave a slow nod of acknowledgment. "As I was going to say, I had no intention of doing any such thing." Not that he could steal it even if he wanted to. This attack had happened on the sheriff's turf. Literally. Made the case personal for them. It was personal for him as well, but Mel didn't want anyone to know that, which he'd respect.

"Good," Holden said. "Then you're welcome to stay."

Thanks for your permission. He was staying whether Holden liked it or not.

"But we've got this well in hand," Holden added.

Waylon stepped deeper into the room. "No doubt in my mind you do. I'm here informally."

The chief deputy's gaze swung back to Melanie. "Did the assailant say anything to you? Threaten you? Indicate what he wanted?"

She shook her head. "No, he didn't."

"Not in the garage where he first attacked you," Holden said, "or here in the offices? Anything?"

"As a matter of fact, not a single word from him."

Holden made a note in his pad. "And when you managed to get his visor up, you didn't get a look at him at all? Could you see his skin color? Was he white, Black, Hispanic? What about his eye color?"

Taking a breath, Melanie shook her head again. "I don't know. Sorry. I tried to identify him, to get a sample of his DNA, but he had the visor glued shut. It took everything to get it up half an inch." Her gaze fell to the trembling hand in her lap.

Her fingernails were broken and bloody, her knuckles bruised. A bad scrape on her knee looked tender and when the EMT cleaned the wound, Melanie flinched.

Waylon could only imagine how terrified she must've been, how hard she had fought to survive.

"After I got the visor to budge a little, it only enraged him. That's when he hit me." She gestured to her face, moved the ice pack from her left cheek and pressed it to the back of her head, giving him a good look at her.

A nasty bruise had already formed on her brown cheek. The ice had done little to prevent swelling. Blood oozed from a cut on her lower lip and a black eye was blooming. He reckoned she was going to have one heck of a shiner in an hour or two.

Fury pierced Waylon deeply, taking root in a dark place inside him he seldom acknowledged. Melanie had taken brutal blows, but she hadn't gone down without a fight—fueled by fear and adrenaline, he supposed.

Weariness and pain glimmered in her eyes, right along with

strength and determination. Tonight, he could've lost her forever. Regardless of whether they were together in some ca-
pacity, Melanie was a bright light meant to shine and do so
much good. The world would be a darker place without her.

He swore under his breath and swallowed around the lump
of raw emotion lodged in his throat. The need to tear apart
whoever had dared to hurt her surged through him, but he
tamped it down.

"Any identifying marks?" Holden asked.

"He was completely covered. Helmet. Long sleeves. Gloves."

"Did you smell anything on him?" Waylon treaded closer.
"Aftershave? Alcohol? Weed?"

Shooting him a fierce glance, Holden heaved a breath.

"Uh, yeah, I did." She nodded. "Cigarette smoke. Menthol."

"How can you be sure it was menthol?" the chief deputy
asked.

Her father was a smoker. A bad habit she tried to get him
to break.

"A guy I knew in Denver only smoked menthols. We spent
a lot of time together. Sometimes the smell would get into my
clothes."

They'd spent a lot of time together in close proximity if the
smell had permeated her clothing. News to him.

A lot about Melanie he longed to know, but only a brief
window had opened after they'd made love when she'd been
willing to share. If she had to work the next day, once the sun
rose, she threw on clothes, had coffee, and either kicked him
out of her house or skedaddled from his place.

They'd been doing that tango for almost three years. One
night a week had turned into three, sometimes four. Strictly
sex had shifted to takeout beforehand, cuddling afterward,
along with pillow talk—a sure sign that things had been more
than physical, coffee together in the mornings and a few hur-

ried kisses. Some holiday weekends they'd spent several days in a row together.

Fed up with the bare minimum, he'd finally pushed for a real relationship. He'd wanted to go out to dinner, hold her hand in public, take a vacation, wake up every day with her. Discuss their future.

The sex was off the charts. No woman did it for him the way she did. But he'd wanted more.

She hadn't, and had ended it. Lectured him about professional boundaries. Spouted bad-timing mumbo jumbo in a rather cold and impersonal manner, like she was delivering a closing argument in a courtroom, without bothering to give him a chance at a rebuttal.

Deep down, he suspected she simply didn't want distractions from her job and was willing to burn any bridge to make district attorney.

Maybe she'd burned one too many bridges in Denver.

"Did the relationship end badly?" Waylon asked, eliciting another sigh from the chief deputy.

"It did." Melanie hung her head. "It's one of the reasons I moved here from Denver." The EMT bandaged her leg and she winced. "But he wouldn't do this."

"Are you sure?" Holden asked and she nodded.

Waylon stepped within easy reach of her. "What's his name?"

Melanie stiffened, avoiding any eye contact.

"Give *me* his name," Holden said, throwing him a scathing glare. "*I'll* have a chat with him, feel him out. That way we can be sure and eliminate him as a possible suspect."

"That won't be necessary. You don't need his name." Her tone changed, the unyielding ADA coming through. "He isn't violent and has no reason to physically hurt me," she said to Holden. "He was glad when I left Denver and we've had no contact since. Except for an email he sent me, a couple of years ago. An invitation to an event, which I declined to attend. This wasn't him."

Physically struck Waylon. This guy might want to hurt her emotionally. Or maybe she'd been the one hurt in the fallout of the relationship.

"Okay." Holden pressed his lips in a firm line. "Has anyone made any threats against you lately? Have you received any hate mail?"

Convicted felons sometimes said reckless things after sentencing, but he wasn't aware of anything recent, and he made it his business to keep track.

"Nothing. It's been quiet." Her delicate shoulders hunched. "Until tonight."

Another deputy pushed past the other two, entering the room, holding a tablet. "The perp waited two hours for her." Deputy Platt turned the screen toward them and tapped it, playing back the surveillance footage from one of the security cameras.

Melanie got up from the chair and came over, standing between them. Her gaze fell to the tablet as her hand held the ice pack lower.

He looked at the side of her jaw. Swollen and quickly turning purple. His gut clenched as he imagined a meaty fist connecting with her face.

She stepped closer to him, on purpose or unconsciously, shifting his focus.

Waylon took in the scent of her. Jasmine and musk and something else warm particular to her. Whenever they'd been together at his place, he hadn't washed his sheets immediately, just to hold on to the smell of her for as long as he could.

Their fingers brushed, the slight touch sending a spark shooting through him.

She moved her hand away, putting the cold compress back up to her face.

He guessed the contact had been purely accidental. But the proximity to Mel pulled at his emotions, a dangerous thing in a room full of people. He turned his attention back to the surveillance footage. Away from Melanie and the need he felt for her.

They watched the perp creep up the garage ramp, hugging the wall, to the third level. Helmet on. Gloves. Sneakers. He glanced at the cameras, like he already knew their locations, and made a beeline for her SUV. Dropping down on the side, out of view of the camera, he stayed there a moment and then crept over to one of the concrete pillars.

"Wonder why he decided to move so far away from her SUV and stopped there instead of hiding closer?" Holden said as if thinking aloud.

"Because of the position of the other two vehicles beside the ADA's still in the lot." Waylon pointed to them. "One of the drivers might have spotted him as they left."

The perp ducked down behind the pillar, taking a seat on the ground. From that angle, with the low wall of the parking ramp that curved around as a shield, he was completely blocked from the view of the camera. The helmet lifted—he must've removed it, but they couldn't even see the top of his head to refine the description of who they were looking for.

Seconds later, a thin trail of smoke wafted up in the air from his position.

"He planned this out carefully," Waylon said. "Knew exactly where to hide and brought cigarettes to smoke while he waited. You need to have your deputies check the spot for cigarette butts and review all the footage for the last two or three weeks. Look for anyone scoping out the place, monitoring Mel—Merritt's—comings and goings."

"I know how to do my job," Holden said, the words emerging like a sigh. He looked at the deputies lingering in front of the door. "Go take care of it, will you?" He turned the tablet toward them, showing them where to look.

Cody hurried off down the hall.

Waylon would've apologized to Holden, but he wasn't sorry. He didn't care if he stepped on someone else's toes. This wasn't simply any case.

"I have no doubts about your competency or that of your department," Waylon said. "I just want to get this SOB. A dedicated detective should be helping you on this one." They were experts, after all, and unlike the sheriff's department, they wouldn't have their focus spread thin by everything else going on in the entire county. This sort of thing would put a squeeze on their resources. The sheriff's department didn't even have the budget to keep crime scene investigators on staff. A handful of deputies had taken some training courses, making them capable of handling routine things such as thefts and burglaries. But their most experienced person, who had worked homicides, had been killed recently. "Maybe Hannah Delaney, Kent Kramer or Brian Bradshaw." All were excellent and, more importantly, he trusted them.

"I'll give it consideration," Holden said. "Run the idea by the sheriff in the morning." He fast-forwarded the footage.

The perp finished smoking and put the helmet back on. The district attorney, Gordon Weisman, had left a half hour later. At nine, one of the paralegals he recognized, Rosenfeld, walked out while talking on the phone. The young woman popped her trunk and rummaged around in the back for several minutes, engrossed in her conversation. No clue the guy was there, lurking only a few feet away. The woman hung up and climbed into her car.

Mel left the offices. She marched over to the trash can, hesitated a moment, and threw away the flowers.

Waylon snuck a furtive look her way that she ignored without even a glance in his direction.

"Who were the flowers from?" Holden asked, pausing the playback, and Deputy Platt lowered the tablet.

"No one important," she said, her tone nonchalant. She tucked loose strands behind her ear, like a nervous habit.

He'd never seen the formidable Melanie Merritt nervous. Except for when he'd admitted his feelings for her.

"The guy is just an ex," she added, still fiddling with her hair. "Not even that. Simply someone I saw from time to time to scratch an itch, if you know what I mean, before I decided to end the dalliance."

No one important. Scratch an itch. Dalliance.

The words stung, wounding his heart more than his ego.

"The name of this spurned lover?" Holden held his pen, waiting for an answer.

"I never said spurned."

"Maybe he didn't like you ending things," Holden said. "Maybe the message didn't sink in. Could be a situation where if he couldn't have you then no one could."

Waylon restrained a groan and swore to himself. He was about to make the list of suspects.

"He's a good guy," she said. "Not the perp you're after. Trust me."

The chief deputy folded his arms across his chest. "For a victim, you sure are reluctant to give us the names of these two men who could be responsible," he said and her chin jerked up at that. "Nothing I can do about identifying Mr. Denver without your assistance. But Mr. Flowers is a different story. If there's a card from the shop out on the ground, it might have his prints."

Another curse prickled Waylon's tongue. It definitely had his prints.

"In the event it doesn't," Holden continued, "he probably used a credit card to pay for the flowers, or someone will remember him buying such an extravagant bouquet. We'll track him down with or without your cooperation, though I'd prefer the former."

Melanie pivoted, facing the chief deputy. "You're barking up the wrong tree. Any time you invest in looking into him is a waste. You should focus on anyone who seemed like they were surveilling the garage or monitoring my comings and goings, like Detective Wright suggested. Whoever attacked me obviously knew I leave late every night."

"Excuse me, ma'am," Cody said, coming back into the room, his hand outstretched. Her designer purse and leather laptop straps dangled from his fingers and her shoe was in his other hand. "Here you go. You can have these back now, and your wallet is in there."

"So, this wasn't a mugging." Waylon looked between Holden and Melanie. "I'm guessing that purse is worth a few hundred dollars." Not that he needed to guess. She'd spent more on some of her handbags than most folks in the area did on the monthly mortgage for their house. "And he didn't bother with your wallet. He targeted you and attacked you for some other reason."

Deputy Cody turned to Holden. "There were no cigarette butts in the spot where he hid. Only ash on the ground."

"If he was smart enough to pick it up and take it with him," Waylon said, "then surely he didn't send her flowers that could be traced back to him."

Holden frowned and it was obvious by the way his mouth twitched that the chief deputy was biting his tongue.

Melanie slipped on her second shoe. "Can I go now?" She stashed the ice pack in her purse. "If there are any other questions, I think it can wait until tomorrow. Don't you agree?"

Holden glanced past her at the EMT. "Is she medically cleared?"

"Are you sure you don't want to go get checked out at the hospital?" the tech asked.

She turned her attention to the EMT. "I'm good. Really. I need to get home."

"It's entirely possible you could have a concussion," the paramedic said.

"No blurred vision. No nausea. Or confusion. Or dizziness. If something changes, I'll go to the hospital. Right now, a trip to the emergency room is the last thing I want. I'm leaving."

The EMT shrugged and shut the lid to the first-aid kit. "I can't force you to take reasonable precautions, ma'am. You're cleared to leave if you want."

"I'll give you a ride home," Waylon said to her.

Melanie looked surprised. Then guarded. "Thanks, but I can drive myself."

"Afraid not, ma'am," Deputy Platt said.

Mel's brow furrowed. "Why is that?"

"When the perp dropped out of view on the side of your car, he flattened two tires," Waylon said. They had been slashed down to the rims. "He made sure you weren't going anywhere."

"We can give you a ride to your house," Holden said before Waylon had a chance to.

"No, no, that won't be necessary." She hitched her purse and laptop bag on her shoulder. "You all have better things to do and it's late. I'll call for a rideshare. I'm fine."

Mel could be stubborn, but this wasn't the time for her obstinate independence.

"It is *late*, and you are *not* fine. You were just assaulted." Waylon marveled at her fierce determination to want to go home alone, in the dark, after what she had gone through. "I'm off duty." Which was relative. For him, he was always working. "I'll make sure you get home safely. Frees up the deputies so they can get back to work finding the guy who did this to you." He gave her an unflinching look to let her know this was nonnegotiable and stressed, "Let's go." He extended his arm and waited for her to walk out first.

Her gaze narrowed, always a lawyer up for a fight, and he braced for her to debate the matter. Whether she liked it or not, she would be driven home. By him.

With an annoyed shake of her head, she left the office without protest.

In the hall, he came up beside her but didn't say anything until they had cleared the busted door. "Mel—"

She raised her palm, cutting him off. "Not here, Detective, and for the record, I'm capable of deciding how I get home."

Not wanting to argue, he walked her to his compact truck and unlocked the door. His GMC Sonoma was an older model that sat lower to the ground than newer trucks and lacked a running board. Putting his hands on her waist, he gave her a slight boost up inside since she was wearing a tailored slim-fitting skirt that restricted her movements.

Off to the side, he couldn't help noticing the card from the flower shop bagged as evidence.

Maybe it was best to have a frank conversation with Holden and tell him he'd been the former nobody in Melanie's bed. Sooner or later, Holden was going to find out anyway. But Waylon needed her permission first.

He hustled over to his side and took off. Once they cleared the garage, he glanced over at her. "Melanie."

"I know where this conversation is headed, and I don't want to have it."

If she thought he was going to bring up their former relationship, she was wrong. This wasn't the time and/or place for that kind of discussion. His only concern was her well-being and the case. "You've got no idea what I'm going to say."

"Your protective cowboy instincts are in overdrive right now because you have feelings for me."

"Apparently, they're one-sided."

"I didn't say that." She rubbed her temple. "I should've asked the medic for a painkiller for my head."

Waylon leaned over, popping the glove box, and handed her some Tylenol. His attention snagged on how her skirt rode up, exposing a bit of her sexy, toned thighs. Just enough silky-smooth, chestnut-colored skin to scatter his thoughts for a moment.

Clearing his head, he opened the center console and gave her a bottle of water. She dumped two gel capsules into her palm and washed them down with a little water.

"This conversation is going to get heavy. I don't want to say anything that'll hurt you," she said, but too late for that. "Let's not do this right now. Okay?"

She phrased it like a question, as if up for discussion, but that wasn't the case. He was fluent in Mel-speak. She cracked her window several inches, letting in fresh air, and switched on the radio.

The sound of Garth Brooks crooning something about thunder rolling filled the truck cab and the empty space of silence between them.

His intent wasn't to cause more stress. They were going to discuss the way she'd blown up their relationship, but at a different time. Tonight, he only had one more thing that he had to mention. "In the morning, I need to tell Holden about us."

She opened her mouth to object.

"Stop." His voice was soft yet firm. "Listen to me. We both know it won't take him long to figure it out when he traces the flowers. But by then, he won't be the only one to know. The whole department will. I can get him to keep it quiet if I get out in front of it." He was on somewhat good terms with the Powell family these days. After he'd set aside old resentments with Holden's brother Monty and had helped them all out on a mission across the state line, Waylon had earned the right to call in a favor. "I won't unless you agree, but it's the smart thing to do."

Melanie was brilliant. She had an uncanny ability to read people, making her great at picking juries, spoke six different languages, attended a fancy prep school as a teen, went to Harvard and Yale, and was highly respected for her good judgment by most people he knew in law enforcement.

Once she eliminated emotion, she would see that this was the best way to handle it.

Flattening her mouth in a thin line, she simply nodded. "Are you sure he won't say anything?"

"Positive." Waylon frowned at the cut on her lip. When he got his hands on the guy who'd done that to her, he was going to make him regret it before he brought him to justice. There was no way he wasn't working on this case unofficially.

Officially, he needed to have a detective of his choice assigned to her case. The chief of the LPD, Wilhelmina Nelson, trusted his judgment and if anyone could persuade Sheriff Daniel Clark, it was her, considering they were married.

In what felt like no time, they turned down her street. Melanie only lived fifteen minutes away in a house on a cul-de-sac, in a quiet, middle-class neighborhood that had good-sized yards with decent space between the homes.

Waylon parked in the driveway. He was out of his truck and by her passenger's-side door when she stepped onto the asphalt with her bags.

"I'll check inside before you go in," he said.

"If you insist."

"I do." He was grateful she didn't argue with him. They headed for her covered front steps. "I can stay the night if you want," he offered, and she tensed. "On the sofa or in the guestroom, Mel." Goodness, he didn't want her to think he was trying to make a move on her at a time like this. She'd just gone through something traumatic and needed to rest without worry. "It's not good for you to be alone tonight. I'd prefer to be inside instead of sleeping in my truck, parked in your driveway." But he wasn't leaving her alone.

"You should go home." She tucked more strands behind her ear. "I don't need a babysitter, especially not…" Her voice trailed off as she stopped near the steps.

He tore his gaze from her face and looked to see what she was staring at.

On her front stoop, under the portico, there was a circle of sand. Two feet in diameter. In the center was an impression, resembling an angel. Like someone had made it in the sand using a large doll.

"I-I-It can't be," she whispered, her face growing ashen. "It can't be."

"Mel, what are you talking about? Can't be what?"

Shaking her head slowly, she looked terrified. "It's not possible. I made sure he was convicted and put behind bars."

"Who?" Waylon looked back at the front stoop. "What is this?"

"He swore he'd make me pay. Me and everyone else responsible for his conviction." She started trembling. "But he's serving a life sentence in a Colorado prison. It can't be him. He couldn't be the one who attacked me."

Waylon took hold of her shoulders, turning her toward him. "Who are you talking about?" he asked gently.

She swallowed so hard it was audible. "That's his calling card." She pointed back at the stoop while staring at him, her eyes filling with tears. "Drake Colter. The Sand Angel Killer."

Chapter Three

Never-ending.

The night was never-ending, with the horror and the necessary presence of the sheriff's deputies.

She could only presume her masked attacker had left the sand angel on her doorstep as a message for the police. To give them an indication of what would have happened to her if he had been successful.

A shudder slipped through Melanie.

Not a close-call mugging or an assault. The man wearing the helmet had intended to kill her.

He must've planned to incapacitate her, transport her to a different location, a sand dune, where he would've killed her and left her body.

That's what happened to the Sand Angel Killer's victims. The weight of that hit her full-force and she swayed on her feet.

Waylon put a hand to her back, steadying her.

She appreciated him risking the small gesture of comfort, considering Holden was going to find out about them anyway.

"Maybe you should take a break," Waylon said.

Holden had been firing off question after question, and she didn't have any concrete answers.

"No, I want to finish." Better to press through and get it over with, so this night could finally end.

Melanie glanced back over at the sand angel impression by her front door. The knot in the center of her chest tightened.

A deputy finished taking pictures. She was anxious to wrap up and get out of there. No way she'd be able to sleep inside her own house tonight.

"It must be a copycat," she said. Drake Colter, the SAK, was locked up in a supermax prison in Florence, Colorado. Not just any jail, but the most secure prison in the world, often called the Alcatraz of the Rockies. Experts in prison design deemed it to be one hundred percent unescapable. "Someone who admired the Sand Angel Killer and decided to target me for some reason."

"That's what I don't understand," Holden said. "You prosecuted this murderer, Colter, and he was locked up three and a half years ago. Why would someone go after you now?"

The same question ricocheted in her mind.

She gave the chief deputy a weary shrug. Her temples throbbed. The back of her head ached. Her face was sore. She was exhausted, more so mentally and emotionally than physically. "I don't know."

"Do you need another cold compress for your head?" Waylon asked, his warm sturdy hand still on her, making her pulse pound.

"I'll be okay."

When they'd first started spending time together, somehow, with no effort at all, they'd slipped into the same frequency, a special channel for only the two of them, where they could read each other so easily.

Too easily.

Months apart should've destroyed the connection. Diminished it at the very least. Now they were in proximity to each other again, dialed back in and attuned. The prospect of him sensing what she felt or thought unnerved her.

She didn't want him to realize that despite her façade of not needing anyone, she did need him tonight, after the attack on her at the office and this violation at her home.

But that wasn't a door she dared reopen. Too complicated. For them both.

Melanie fought off another wave of dizziness, a bitter bite on her tongue.

"Do you need to sit for a minute?" Waylon's deep voice, a protective growl mixed with concern, pushed at the barrier she'd set between them.

"This has all been a lot." She struggled to maintain her composure, to keep tears from her eyes. Breaking down under emotion wasn't like her at all, but her bruises were fresh, painful, and far more than skin deep. "I need to get cleaned up, catch my breath. Process everything with some quiet." Another ice pack wouldn't hurt, either, but she wanted to leave.

"Okay." Holden nodded, closing his notepad. "I think you've answered my questions for tonight. Too bad we don't have more to go on."

The security camera mounted near her front door had captured the perp. Same guy who had attacked her at her office, wearing a black helmet, making it impossible to identify him. The front side of his vehicle had been in the frame.

Not a motorcycle. A white nondescript van.

None of her neighbors had noticed anything unusual and the use of home security systems in the area was rare. If the neighbor to her right had had one, they would most likely have the license plate number or the make and model.

The bad thing about Laramie and Bison Ridge was the lack of a robust traffic camera system. The ones they had were few and far between, and only at major intersections.

Someone as careful as her assailant would be clever enough to avoid them.

Holden put his notepad away, slipped his pen in his shirt pocket and glanced at the deputies collecting evidence in front of her house. "We'll need to go inside as well. Just to be sure."

She wrapped her arms around herself. Nothing on her security footage indicated that the perp had gone inside, but it was best for them to be sure and check.

"I don't recommend you spend the night here," Holden said.

"I wasn't planning on it."

"And you shouldn't be alone," the chief deputy added.

Waylon dropped his hand from her back, but she was aware that was probably contrary to what he wanted to do. He was an affectionate, emotionally transparent type of guy.

In many ways, they were opposites.

Soon enough, the chief deputy would know that she had been sleeping with Waylon. Still, appearances mattered for the others who were starting to turn their attention toward them.

Her cheeks burned with embarrassment over the impending exposure of their secret.

"She won't be alone," Waylon said. "I'm going to take her somewhere safe."

"And where would that be?" Holden asked.

Melanie and Waylon exchanged furtive glances. He inclined his head in a silent question to her.

Was it okay to tell Holden here rather than waiting until tomorrow?

A different kind of man wouldn't have sought her permission and simply would've done what he thought best regardless of her feelings. Not Waylon. Never.

He was good, decent. Thoughtful.

Melanie gave a little nod of consent and the burn crept down her throat.

Now was as good a time as any for him to talk to Holden about their relationship. Little point in waiting.

"Do you mind if she goes inside her house to grab a few personal items?" Waylon asked, redirecting the conversation to her surprise.

"It would be better to wait until after we've finished up,"

Holden said and looked at her. "You might want to just come back in the morning."

Melanie nodded. "That's fine."

"I need to speak to you for a minute," Waylon said to Holden. "Privately. Let me get the ADA inside my truck first."

"Sure." Holden traipsed behind them, giving them space.

Relief eased a bit of tension from her shoulders. Waylon intended to do it one-on-one, sparing her from the conversation and the in-your-face humiliation of having her personal life revealed.

She slid a glance at Waylon, catching his eye. "Thank you," she whispered.

"I'll take care of it. Cop-to-cop, cowboy-to-cowboy, is better anyway." His voice was low and reassuring. "You've been through enough tonight."

Waylon helped her climb up into his old truck, shut the door and then he pulled the chief deputy aside.

The two men stopped out of earshot of the other deputies and away from her direct line of sight.

Looking in the side mirror, she could see them and, thanks to the open window in the truck and their proximity, she could also hear them.

"Holden, I need to ask a favor of you."

"Well, that's a first. Waylon Wright asking a favor from a Powell. Sure, what is it?"

Flicking a quick glance at the others working the crime scene, Waylon crossed his arms over his chest and looked back at the chief deputy. "You don't need to dig into the guy who sent ADA Merritt the flowers."

"Why is that?" Holden asked quickly before Waylon finished.

"Because it was me."

Holden put his hands on his hips. "Come again?"

Melanie fidgeted with her hands, wishing Waylon had never

sent those extravagant flowers. Even though they'd been beautiful and the gesture undeniably sweet.

"We've been seeing each other," Waylon said. "Discreetly. Or rather, we were until she called it off. She would prefer it if no one else knew. We would both appreciate it if you could keep it quiet. Not tell anyone else."

Holden scratched his chin, mulling it over. "I guess I can do that. Keep the flowers out of the report. Not as if you were the one who attacked her. But I will need to let the sheriff know. Only him, though, and he won't say anything."

Holden's boss was also his brother-in-law. Small town.

The exception seemed more than reasonable to Melanie, and she released the breath that she had been holding.

"Thank you," Waylon said.

She planned to share her appreciation as well later.

"It's not a big ask on your part, considering you put your life on the line to help my family last year. We needed assistance, off-the-book, and you were there. That's not something that'll soon be forgotten," Holden said.

Melanie had also helped with the awful situation, completely by accident. She'd gone from thinking she might have to bring Monty Powell up on charges of murder, to helping Holden's eldest brother and Waylon—the lead detective—crack the case and identify the person responsible for Monty's troubles.

The circumstances had spiraled, turning deadly, and Waylon had jumped right into the fray, joining their mission. No hesitation. No questions asked. The Powells had needed help and Waylon had been there for them.

She'd been so thankful he had come back unharmed.

Then, only a couple of weeks later, on Christmas, everything between them changed and she'd had to end it.

"So," Holden said, "when you say you're taking her somewhere safe, I assume you mean to your place and that you'll be the one keeping her company."

Waylon nodded. "I do."

Melanie stiffened. She wanted protection, and if she were being honest with herself, also comfort. No one was better suited than Waylon, but she wasn't foolish enough to assume it would be a good idea to accept either from him.

People always disappointed her, failed her in some way eventually. Her biological father acted like she didn't exist. Even her mom and stepdad, whom she considered her real dad, let her down time and time again. The only person she could ever rely on was herself.

"No need to mention that she'll be staying at my place to anyone else," Waylon said. "Besides the sheriff."

The bed-and-breakfast in town would be more than adequate. That's where she was going to spend the night. Not under the same roof as Waylon Wright.

"I appreciate you telling me. Saves time and resources investigating Mr. Flowers. Well, you. It also explains why you showed up tonight. Truth be told, I found your presence at my crime scene particularly irksome, but I get it now. Whether you two are broken up or not. If it had been Grace," Holden said, bringing up his wife, "who'd been attacked and it was your crime scene, I would've been there. Probably getting in the way, trying to take over and give orders, too. No hard feelings." Holden shook Waylon's hand. "My gut tells me this guy who attacked her, whoever he is, Sand Angel Killer serving a life sentence, or more likely some nut-job copycat that left the sand on her front stoop, might try again."

After seeing the sand angel at her home, Melanie's instinct was telling her the same thing.

"I figured that, too," Waylon said.

"The ADA might need a bodyguard until we catch this guy."

"She's got one. Nothing is more important than her safety. Let us know if you find anything inside her house."

"Will do." Holden rejoined the other deputies.

The sheriff's department was going to have an even longer night ahead of them.

Waylon climbed into his truck and started it up. The engine always rattled the first few seconds, like it might give up and die, then purred as though it would run forever.

"You can take me to the bed-and-breakfast in town." She had stayed there for three months when she'd relocated to Laramie from Denver and waited to close on her house. The owners, Mr. and Mrs. Quenby, were a lovely couple and provided free breakfast. "The place is clean and comfortable. Close to my job. It's fine for a week or two."

"No, it's not."

"Yes, it is. The B and B is homey. I'd prefer to stay there. I insist." Melanie gave him one of the long lingering stares she'd realized made most men stutter and back down.

Waylon merely stared back at her. "I'm taking you to my house." He threw the truck in Reverse and backed out of her driveway.

"That's not a good idea or what I want."

Hitting the road, he took off. "Are we really going to do this?"

"Do what?"

He sighed, taking the road that led to Wayward Bluffs, where he lived, rather than heading back into town.

"You're going the wrong way," she said.

"Am I?" His voice was tight. "Because I believe this is the correct way to my house."

She folded her arms. "If you don't take me to the Quenbys' B and B, I'll simply call a rideshare to take me." Going to his house wouldn't put her in the detached headspace she needed to be in to rally. His cozy cabin was filled with memories—passionate, steamy, sweet memories—that would only bring unwelcome emotions to the surface. She was on the verge of cracking when she needed to pull herself together. Being in his home would be hard, but then he'd touch her and she'd fall to pieces. Having a relapse with him, falling back into bed, making love to him, would feel incredible in the moment. Like a junkie getting what they craved. But the sun would rise, along with her shame and regret and anger at herself for being weak. "You have two choices." She spoke with the right amount of conviction, but underneath her confidence was a twinge of anxiety. "Turn around or I pull up the app and request a ride."

"The B and B isn't safe. This guy has been watching you. We have no idea for how long. When you go back to work, he can follow you to the B and B. Book a room. Pretend to be a guest to see which one you're staying in. From there, it would be simple to pop the lock, which isn't a dead bolt, while you're sleeping and finish what he started. Heck, he doesn't even have to go to the trouble of getting a room. All he has to do is watch you go inside and wait to see which room light turns on shortly thereafter."

Icy fear scuttled up her spine and froze her brain.

"This is a small town," Waylon added, "usually so safe and quiet that Mr. and Mrs. Quenby didn't put on a proper lock that's only accessible to guests on the exterior upper door. The perp could get inside in less than sixty seconds guaranteed. If necessary, he might kill the Quenbys, too, or any other guest there to make sure no one hears you scream. Staying at the B and B alone leaves you vulnerable. It's one of the worst places for you to be."

Fighting off a shiver, she clenched her hands. The grim reality of the situation had her rethinking her stance. "I hadn't thought of that."

"You're not a cop or ultra paranoid, why would you?"

Waylon was only looking out for her. As always. "I just don't want you to get the wrong idea about us. We're simply friends now. That's all we can be." If she cared anything about her job, about advancement and realizing her professional dream, he needed to stay off limits.

"Mel, this isn't a romantic overture. I'm only taking you to my house for your safety."

"This is a big deal, Waylon. I'm the ADA. You're a detective. I can't be shacked up with you."

"We're not shacking up. It's protective custody." His grip tightened on the steering wheel. "You're used to controlling everything and all situations. But this is something you can't control. As a prosecutor, you rely on the expertise of others on a regular basis. Use mine now. Don't think of me as your ex. Only as a professional who also happens to be your friend. Let me keep you safe and stop fighting me. Can you do that until we figure out what's going on and put a stop to it?"

She was fighting their chemistry, his raw sexual magnetism, an attraction to him still as strong as ever, and her desire for something with him that she couldn't have, more than she was fighting him.

Not that he would appreciate the distinction.

Her whole career, she had never been anything *but* careful. Until she'd gotten involved with Waylon Wright.

Melanie drew in a ragged breath. "I can try."

Chapter Four

Once they made it to Wayward Bluffs, the knot at the base of Waylon's spine still hadn't loosened. Melanie's situation was even more dire than he'd first feared.

Keeping her safe was all that mattered.

By the time he got Melanie settled inside his house, it was after midnight. Waylon had to restrain the impulse to physically comfort her. A hard thing to do considering what she'd endured.

The shower started running in the one full bathroom he had in the log-sided home. He lived a good thirty-minute drive from Laramie. The one-story place sat on four acres and had expansive views in every direction with the mountains to the north.

Peaceful and priceless in his opinion.

The funny thing was, he never would've met Mel—not ADA Merritt—if he hadn't lived in Wayward Bluffs. He'd trudged into Crazy Eddie's, the little honky-tonk bar two miles down the road from his house. Hunger had driven him there without showering, shaving or putting on fresh clothes after spending the entire day painting his kitchen and living room. Friday night. Famished. Ordered a beer and burger. Ready to unwind to some good music. Not really interested in much else.

She had sidled up on the bar stool next to him, the scent of her perfume registering along with her presence. "Drinking alone?" she'd asked in a sultry voice.

He'd cast a glance at her and been awestruck.

Leggy, big-breasted blondes were his usual go-to. Uncomplicated gals who didn't expect much from him since he had a demanding job and modest lifestyle, but this woman was the opposite.

Petite. Dark hair. A warm, smooth, brown complexion. Sophisticated.

Nothing basic about her.

And way out of his league.

Taking off his cowboy hat and setting it on the other stool, he smiled at her, his attention roving over her lithe frame from the front of her light blue sweater that hugged a nice set of breasts, trim waist, down her lean legs clad in tight-fitting jeans and to the sexiest strappy black heels.

"Not if you join me," he said, and she turned slightly so that her thigh brushed up against his. And just that light touch sent excitement coiling deep inside him. "New to the area?"

He'd never seen her around before and certainly would've noticed this lovely lady.

"Sort of. Just moved to the great Cowboy State, but I'm about thirty minutes away."

That could put her in Laramie, Bison Ridge, Centennial or Cheyenne, which was in an entirely different county. "What brings you to Wayward Bluffs?"

She flipped her hair over her shoulder, kicking up that enticing, expensive scent. "I don't want to start anything with someone in my backyard, if you know what I mean."

He raised a brow. "But you're interested in starting something with me?"

"I am," she said with suggestion, "provided we can reach an understanding."

Boy oh boy, he loved her confidence. And she was a beauty. Too beautiful for him. Glossy raven hair. A killer body. She looked like a shorter, slightly younger version of Freida Pinto, the actress, and she had the most direct personality he'd ever encountered.

No woman had ever picked him up. Especially not one drop-dead gorgeous. He was a big guy. Six-five. Two hundred forty pounds. His build was intimidating. Something he was cognizant of around women and did his best never to do anything to make them uneasy, but she didn't act the least bit daunted.

"I'm all ears." He took a sip of his beer, tapping his foot to the beat of the music the band played.

"My terms. I say when. I say where." She shifted on her stool, sliding her knee along the inside of his, cozying up even more to him. "Let's start with one night. No last names. See how it goes." Dark eyes teasing and hot, she gave a smile that could wound.

He did his best to keep from grinning like a fool, but he felt as though he'd won the lottery. Strange. He was a serial monogamist and had never had a one-night stand.

But he'd take whatever he could get with this woman.

"What do you think?" she asked. "Are you game, cowboy?"

Yes. Yes. Yes! "I'm your huckleberry."

That smile of hers spread, knocking the breath from his lungs. "There's a motel not far from here."

The bartender, Steve, set his food down on the bar top in front of him.

"I know the one," Waylon said and nodded his thanks to Steve. "But my house is closer and free."

She swiveled and looked at the bartender. "Do you know this fellow?"

"Yeah, sure do," Steve replied, having full knowledge of him and his family since they'd both grown up in the area. "That's Waylon—"

"I don't need to know his last name, as long as you do, in the event a woman fitting my description turns up missing.

Would you say a lady, such as myself, would be safe in his company, alone?"

"With him?" Steve pointed a finger at Waylon and grinned. "No one safer you could pick in this bar, lady."

Waylon tipped his head to the bartender for such a strong endorsement.

"Thank you," she said, and Steve went to help another customer. "You're not a convicted felon are you, Waylon?"

Chuckling, he choked on his beer. "No, ma'am."

"Don't 'ma'am' me unless you're looking to kill the vibe. My name is Melanie. Are you involved with anyone, romantically, sexually, emotionally?"

That was *very* specific. "If this is only a one-night-at-a-time sort of thing, does it really matter to you?" He picked up the burger and bit into it.

"It does. I don't want to step on any toes and I'm not fond of cheaters."

She had amazing skin. Radiant. Smooth. All natural besides a bit of lip gloss. Hands down the sexiest thing about her was that bold, distinctive style of hers.

Waylon swallowed his food. "Lucky for you, I'm free and clear," he said and she studied him with keen interest as though she could detect a lie. "No entanglements on any of those counts." But he was interested in having one with her. "I hope it's the same with you."

He didn't mess with women who weren't available. Not even for a night.

She gave a little nod. "The same."

This was his lucky night. "Hey, how do you know I'm not lying?"

For all she knew, he could be a married cheater not wearing his wedding ring, or even a serial killer. There was that phenomenon where friends and relatives claimed the murderer was such a nice guy that they never suspected.

"I can tell," she said and, for some reason, he believed her. "Besides, you've got an honest vibe to you. Something about the way you carry yourself drew me to you."

"So, it wasn't my good looks that caught your attention." He chuckled again. From a distance, some women probably found him attractive, but up close, when they got a good look at the faint scars he still had from an accident as a teenager, he was aware his lack of a pretty-boy face wasn't for everyone.

"It was also your big hands." She winked at him.

Another chuckle rolled from his mouth despite trying to play it cool. He couldn't remember the last time or any time a woman had made him smile much less laugh.

She started to stand. "Let's go."

"Mind if I finish eating first, darling?"

"But I'm ready. Now." Her tone indicated she didn't apologize for what she wanted when she wanted it. "You understand I'm offering a night of fun, no-strings attached?"

"I do." He squirted ketchup all over his French fries. "But it's been a long day and I'm starving." He stuffed a few fries in his mouth.

Looking surprised, she plopped her behind back down on the stool.

This woman was used to getting her way. He had the feeling that after one night, he'd be wrapped around her little finger, but he couldn't make it too easy for her.

First impressions counted, lasted. She struck him as the type that enjoyed a bit of a challenge.

"They have takeout containers." She rested her elbow on the bar. "You could eat on the way."

"I don't like to get the inside of my truck dirty. Pet peeve."

"I suppose that's that a good thing. You know what they say about cleanliness." She sighed and even the sound of her irritation was hot. "If you're going to make me wait, you had better be worth my time."

"I've never had any complaints." He took another bite of the burger.

"Just because you haven't had any complaints doesn't mean the women were pleased with your performance. Maybe they didn't want to hurt your feelings or were afraid to speak the truth."

No danger of that with this one. Direct Mel wouldn't hesitate to hurt him in an effort to be honest. Of that, he was certain.

"Let me clarify. I always get rave reviews." He crammed some more fries in his mouth, chewed and swallowed. "But I can tell you're not easy to please, so I'll do my extra best." He definitely wanted to leave her craving more so he could see her again.

"Would you mind hurrying up?" she asked with a hint of a scowl.

He put a hand on her knee, stroked up her thigh to her hip. "I hope you don't aim to rush me in the bedroom, darling." He took a massive bite of his burger, practically inhaling his dinner. As much as he wanted to pique her interest by not appearing overly eager, he sensed a fine line with this one and was just as enthusiastic about getting her back to his place.

She leaned in close. Her soft floral scent curled around him in odd contrast to her sharp appeal. She picked up a napkin and wiped his mouth. "In the bedroom, I expect you to take your time. Make the most of the entire night. Bonus points if you can get me to scream your name."

Oh yeah, she was going to be fun. "I do like extra credit." To heck with finishing his meal. He pulled money from his wallet, dropped it on the bar, and put his hat on her head. She looked good wearing his Stetson. He couldn't wait to see it on her with those sexy heels and nothing else. "I'm definitely the right cowboy for you."

Looking back on it, after she had discovered he was a detective with the LPD, which meant they'd have to work together from time to time, and she'd still wanted to see him, he should have set down some of his own ground rules.

Instead, he'd made the mistake of doing it her way, on her terms, for almost three years.

The shower stopped and he waited for her in the hall.

She opened the door and stepped out, wearing one of his T-shirts that fell to her knees. A surge of awareness jump-started parts of him that needed to stay idle. Warm eyes centered on him and the world dropped out from under him. Her golden-brown complexion spoke of her Indian heritage and the bruises on her face were prominent. He ached to hold her.

A shuddering breath left her. "I understand why staying at the bed-and-breakfast in town wasn't a wise idea." Pushing her damp hair back behind her ears with trembling hands, she looked so delicate. "But I don't want to make things awkward between us."

Her distress was palpable. Understandable. What she'd experienced left survivors traumatized. PTSD as a result of an assault was common.

Looking at her, he'd forgotten just how fragile a strong woman could be.

"You need to be someplace familiar. Somewhere you feel safe. And definitely not alone." He crossed the space between them in two long strides, drew her up against him, and held her close.

Mel stiffened and a tremble racked her body.

At five-five, with no heels on, the top of her head only came to his chest. She was so small, so slender in his arms. But warm and soft, vibrant and *alive*.

Thank God, she'd gotten away from her assailant.

"No matter what, I'm here for you. As a friend, if that's all you want." Though he wanted to be so much more. "You don't have to be the strong, impervious ADA. Not with me. Whatever you need, M&M, I've got you. Always."

Going pliant, she melted into his embrace, gripped the back of his shirt, and buried her face in his chest. With her head tucked snugly under his chin, everything inside him quieted. She held him tight, her fingers curling into the fabric.

They stayed like that, silent, still, with him holding her for a long time until her breath came in ragged spurts. Her chest heaved against him and she cried. Gut-wrenching, muffled sobs. Tears rolled down her cheeks, leaving damp trails on his shirt in their wake. A barrier had come down. Something so elementary as him offering a warm hug had unraveled her.

The simple gesture of trust resonated through him—the act more powerful than any words. Mel's acceptance of his protection and comfort lit a spark of warmth in his chest. The one hopeful spot in this otherwise dreadful night.

She burrowed closer, her warmth seeping through his clothes.

Every inch of him thrummed with desire. It took all his willpower to keep the contact to only an embrace. He drew a deep breath, inhaling the scent of her damp hair. The tightness in his chest loosened. He'd missed her so much. The indulgence of this hug brought him some small measure of solace.

She raised her head from his chest and stared up at him.

He nearly flinched at the raw pain and vulnerability in her eyes, but he forced himself not to react because it would only cause her to retreat.

Bringing his hand to cup her face, he brushed his thumb over her cheek, repeating the slow motion not only to console her but because he needed this contact. Although he wanted to be her rock, her anchor, during this storm, she soothed something restless deep inside him. Brightened the darkest parts of his life, just by being near him.

"I didn't want you to bring me to your house, but… Thank you. I'm glad I'm here with you now." Her breath flowed warm across his chin, a soft caress. "Tomorrow, I need to go to Florence, Colorado. To the prison and see him face-to-face. Drake Colter," she said, referring to the Sand Angel Killer. The supermax prison was more than a five-hour drive, two hours south of Denver. "Find out if he might know anything about a possible copycat who could be after me. I can do it by myself, but I'd rather not. Colorado is a difficult place for me to go back to. Would you take me? If you can't," she added quickly, without giving him a chance to respond, "I understand. It'd be a last-minute day off for you. I'm sure you have better things to do with your time. Or there's a case you're working on. I'll be fine on my own."

The woman of steel who never asked for help wanted his. "Of course. I wouldn't let you go by yourself."

"*Let* me? At a later date, we should discuss this antiquated and ridiculous notion that you have the power to allow or disallow anything I do."

No need to ever have that chat.

"I misspoke. I can't stop you, but I would've pushed to go with you." He was pleased he didn't have to, and that she'd asked. "I'll call the chief." He needed to talk to her about assigning a detective to the case anyway. "Take a few personal days." He had a ton saved. His intent had been to spend a week with her on the beach somewhere on vacation. The romantic suggestion had sent her scrambling for the hills like he'd invited her to get shipwrecked on a deserted island with no hope of a rescue. "It won't be a problem. I just wrapped up a case."

"I appreciate you doing this." She gave him a sad smile, her eyes still glistening with tears.

His gaze fell to her mouth. The perfect, defined bow of her upper lip. The luscious fullness of her lower lip. He loved the way she chewed on it when she was concentrating and didn't think anyone was looking. Even bruised, she was the most beautiful woman he'd ever seen.

Sensations swept through him, battering his control. It'd been too long since he'd been this close to her, held her, kissed her, but he didn't dare overstep. Not when she was scared and vulnerable and needed to feel safe.

Releasing her, he stepped back and took a deep breath to clear his head.

"I made up the guest room for you." After Melanie had complained about the presence of the gun safe in the corner of his bedroom dampening the mood, he'd moved it to the guest room. He worried the sight of the safe, looming in the corner, might make her uneasy, but it was a small house with limited options. "I didn't want to assume you'd be comfortable in my bedroom. With me. Even though I'd be on my best behavior. You've got my word as a cowboy. No line will be crossed tonight. Not even if you begged." The vow brought a smile to her face that reached her eyes and filled him with warmth. A tough promise to keep, but he would. "You wouldn't need to worry."

"I've known that about you since the first night I met you. That I wouldn't need to worry. It's the reason I risked going home with a perfect stranger. I'd prefer to be in your room."

Didn't mean she wanted to be in there with him. "I can take the guest room if you want."

"No need." She pressed her palms to his chest. "Could I ask another favor, as just a friend, since you've given me such solid assurances as a cowboy?"

"Name it."

"Would you mind holding me? Just until I fall asleep."

It would be his pleasure. She needed more comfort than a hug in a hallway could give.

"I think I can muster the strength to endure such a hardship." He kissed her forehead, loving the small moments when she lowered the wall, didn't pretend to be invincible and let him see her vulnerability. *His M&M.* Hard and lovely on the outside, but under that picture-perfect exterior, soft and sweet on the inside. First, she'd asked for his help and now for affection. He'd never deny her anything, especially not this. "Like I said, whatever you need."

Chapter Five

The next afternoon, sitting in the passenger's seat of Waylon's truck, Melanie was fuming as they drove through downtown Denver.

"I can't believe Colter was released ten days ago," she said for the hundredth time. Driving to the supermax in Florence had been a complete waste.

"The prison said it was on a technicality, but what kind of colossal error gets a convicted killer, sentenced to life behind bars, suddenly released?" Waylon asked.

"That's what I want to know." She tried calling the Denver district attorney, Brent Becker, the biggest jerk in the world, on his cell phone yet again. "It went straight to voicemail this time." Gritting her teeth, she wanted to punch something or someone but took a deep breath instead. Her cell phone rang. A spark of hope that Brent was finally returning her six calls withered when she looked at the caller ID. "It's my mom. I wonder why she's calling. It's almost one in the morning in Mumbai." Her parents were in India to visit her mother's family and to attend a wedding. "Hi, Mom. What's wrong?"

"You tell me, Mellie. I've had a bad feeling about you all day. Your father keeps saying it's nothing and that you're fine, but I haven't been able to fall asleep."

Causing her parents to worry while they were eight thousand miles away wouldn't do anyone any good, but she didn't want to lie either. "I'm okay. Please don't worry about me."

"It's my job to worry about you. I'm your mother," she said in Marathi, which Melanie had grown up speaking at home.

Her mother was adamant that Mel learned her native tongue, as well as Hindi and English. In college, she'd also picked up French, Italian and Farsi.

"Did anything happen?" Mom asked, segueing back into English.

Melanie weighed her words. "There's always something. You know that."

"What happened?"

If she told her parents the full story, they'd drop everything and fly out to see her. Only for a day or two, where they'd fret endlessly, pressuring her to leave Wyoming, and she'd worry she might be endangering them. The way they took care of her wasn't always in the way she needed. As a teen, they'd sent her to Phillips Exeter Academy, a boarding school that was a top feeder for Harvard, because they'd wanted the freedom to travel. To live unencumbered. Despite how much they'd loved her, how much she'd needed to stay near them as a young teenager, they'd still sent her away. Since then, she'd learned not to be an inconvenience and wouldn't become one now.

"Someone flattened the tires on my car last night at work, but the sheriff's department is involved and investigating the situation."

"Oh no."

"It's fine. That's what triple A is for."

"Vandalism is better than the horrible things I was imagining. I thought you might've been mugged or hurt or worse."

Melanie cringed on the inside. Her mother had some weird sixth sense when it came to her.

"Are you still using the AirTags I gave you?"

"Yes. I sewed an AirTag inside the lining of all my expensive purses and I have one on my keychain." After her mother had been mugged in New York City and the police had never found her beloved Hermès bag, she used extreme caution. "This isn't a good time for me to talk, Mom. I'm in the middle of doing research regarding a prior case." She slid a glance at Waylon, whose gaze was trained on the road, but she was aware he was listening to every word. "I'm with a detective who's been kind enough to help me on his personal time. Please, put your mind at ease. Give Dad and Grandma a hug. Okay."

"If you're sure everything is all right, I'll let you go. Your father is staring at me, giving me that look. You know the one," her mother said, and Melanie could visualize her father's expression. He was British and dispassionately sensible, choosing to make decisions based on hard facts not a bad feeling, which was one thing about him that Melanie loved. "Yes, Freddy, you were right. Mellie is fine. Happy now." Mom sighed. "Dad says hi and that I should be happy, too, but I still have that bad feeling. Like a wriggling knot in my chest." Another sigh. "No, Freddy, it's not indigestion."

Melanie smiled, suddenly missing her parents. She didn't see them often enough. "Love you both. Get some sleep. Enjoy the festivities. I've got to go." She waited for a reply and disconnected. "I hate being dishonest with them."

"You did your parents a kindness. Once we get to the bottom of this and get it resolved, then you can tell them everything." Waylon patted her hand.

The gesture was a comfort that alleviated an inkling of her guilt over her parents while boosting it in equal measure over doing something she'd never expected to do. Ask for help from the man whose heart she'd broken.

The depths of Waylon's kindness, one of the things she loved most about him, never ceased to surprise her.

Last night, he'd been extraordinary. A patient, perfect gentleman. He'd held her close, stroking her hair and back. She'd practically been cocooned by his large frame. Waylon was a big man, the size of a football player. His strong, hard body had been warm against hers, a reassuring haven in the sudden storm that had swept into her world. She'd wanted to kiss him, to lose herself for a moment in his arms, letting him make love to her, but the mixed messages wouldn't have been fair to him. He was a great guy. The best. Not a yo-yo she could yank back and forth on a whim when it suited her.

"Thank you for coming with me today." Not only had he been there for her in a way she didn't deserve after she'd called it quits with him, but he hadn't forced conversation on the long drive and hadn't brought up their relationship. Or rather, the end of it.

Waylon was a fighter. Went after what he wanted, and he'd made it clear he wanted her. It was the reason she stopped returning his calls. The man was persuasive and had filthy pillow talk she missed. Along with his touch and his kisses. And his cuddles.

But she couldn't help savoring this new layer between them, one of comfort, support. It felt tenuous, and oddly special, and she was reluctant to ruin it.

He flashed her a grin. "Not like I was going to let you, I mean," he said, catching himself, "I wouldn't want you to go alone to see a serial killer, and I'd rather it be me than someone else." His attention turned back to the road.

For the briefest moment, she wondered what her parents would think of Waylon. He was not only handsome and gentle, despite being the intimidating size of a bear, but also polite to the point where he could drive her nuts. They'd appreciate his character—honest and humble—and his work ethic. A natural leader who put in almost as many hours as she did and never stopped until the bad guy was behind bars.

There was so much about him to admire.

To love.

"We're here." He passed a line of news vans parked out

front, pulled into the garage of the courthouse and had to go up to the top floor to find a parking spot. "Full house today."

Some days were busier than others but…

"This is unusual," she said. "Something must be going on."

Melanie flipped down the sun visor and checked her face in the vanity mirror. The concealer under her eye was starting to fade and purple bruising peeked through, but the makeup on her cheeks still looked okay. She pulled out the pair of over-sized sunglasses she had tucked inside her purse and slipped them on.

Wearing shades indoors wasn't something she'd normally do, but today was one for exceptions.

They got out of the truck, cleared security, and made their way to the district attorney's office. She waved hello to familiar faces, avoided answering any questions, and tried to ignore the curious stares that were as much for her as Waylon.

Everyone checked out the man next to her. Not that she blamed them. Waylon was huge. Not only tall, but also burly. A solid two-forty, and not the doughy kind. The first night she'd seen him in Crazy Eddie's, he'd snagged her full attention right away. His size was intimidating and appealing in equal measures. He'd flashed the bartender an easy grin. Radiated calm affability. His eyes were warm, honest. Kind. She'd figured if he was interested and single, then he'd be the one.

At least for a night.

Melanie stopped in front of the desk of the DA's receptionist and clasped her hands.

Susan's eyes grew wide as saucers. "Melanie. I didn't expect you to show up here."

"Why not? You've given me the runaround for the last two hours. What was I supposed to do? Sit and wait for Brent to call me back like a good little girl?"

Susan opened her mouth, but no words came out.

"Is he in there?" Melanie pointed to the DA's office.

"No. He's preparing to give a statement to the media." The middle-aged woman had bags under her eyes and looked ten years older than the last time she'd seen her. "That's why he's been unavailable, and his cell is turned off."

"Why is Drake Colter free?" she demanded.

Susan grimaced. "It's a disaster. That's what the press conference is about." The older woman looked at her watch. "It'll start in twenty minutes, at three o'clock, if you care to stay for it."

"I don't want to listen to whatever garbage he's going to feed the press. I want to talk to him. Now."

"Where is he?" Waylon asked.

Susan looked at him, her gaze raking him from his cowboy hat, past his business-casual attire—a blazer, gray T-shirt that stretched taut across his muscular chest and jeans that hung on him in just the right way—down to his boots. "And you are?"

"Detective Waylon Wright." Pulling back his jacket, he flashed the badge that was hooked to his waistband beside his holstered gun. "Please, don't make me ask again, ma'am."

"He's smoking. Running through his speech. Trying to shake his nerves," Susan said, and Melanie should have guessed. "He's having a rough week. This might be the worst day of his life. Wait until after he speaks to the media, will you?"

Oh, poor Brent.

"No," Melanie said with an indignant shake of her head. "I won't wait."

"Still pushy, heartless and selfish as ever, I see." Susan narrowed her eyes and pursed her lips. "They have a name for women like you, but I'm too dignified to use such vulgarity."

Melanie pressed both palms down on her desk and leaned in. "Someone tried to kill me last night, Susan. You'll have to excuse me if I don't have enough sympathy for Brent because he's having a tough week. And whatever vulgar word you're thinking of, I've been called a lot worse by better people and I didn't lose a wink of sleep over it."

Susan reeled back in her chair aghast. "I didn't realize he'd go after you next."

"He who?" Waylon asked.

"The killer," Susan whispered.

"Drake Colter?" The irritation in Waylon's voice only echoed Melanie's. "And what do you mean by 'next'?"

"Everything is such a mess," Susan said. "Judge Babcock, who presided over the Colter case, the witness who testified that his alibi was a lie, Georgia Jenkins, and the one juror—the holdout who caved in the final hour, making the vote unanimous, and gave that primetime interview—Regina Sweeney, were all murdered after Colter was released."

Ice water ran through Melanie's veins, freezing her heart. Three women.

"Why wasn't she notified?" Waylon asked.

Susan shrugged. "I don't know. That's not my area."

Light-headed, Melanie was speechless for the first time in her adult life.

"Why was he released in the first place?" Waylon demanded. "And why hasn't he been arrested again after these new murders?"

"It's complicated." Bewilderment twisted Susan's features, emphasizing her wrinkles. "You have to ask Brent."

"I intend to," Melanie said, finding her voice.

They turned and stalked out of the office space. She led the way to the stairwell, which was the fastest way to a little-known spot where employees could smoke.

"Is it always a circus around this place?" he asked.

"It wasn't when I worked here." Because she had more or less been in charge and hadn't tolerated cluelessness. She hurried down the steps, patting herself on the back for forsaking her typical suit and heels in lieu of jeans and wedge shoes.

"Why did you leave Denver?"

The question blindsided her. "Multiple factors." She glanced at him. "I'm not trying to be evasive. Ask me again, another time, and I'll tell you."

"I'll hold you to that."

No doubt in her mind that he would.

On the first floor, she led him through a maze of hallways to the small courtyard. She spotted Brent. He was pacing back and forth, speaking to himself, smoking.

He usually enjoyed press conferences, a big public platform where he got to take all the credit, but it was evident from the way he waved his hands and his brow furrowed that he dreaded this one.

She shoved through the door and walked outside with Waylon beside her. "Brent."

His head whipped toward her, his eyes widening in surprise. "Melanie? What on earth are you doing here?"

"I was attacked at work last night."

"Not you, too." Brent hung his head and took a drag on his cigarette. "Did the assault make the news?" His green eyes flashed up at them. "Where are you living these days? Wyoming, right?"

The guy hadn't changed. Still despicable.

Waylon stepped toward him. "You should be asking her if she's all right."

"Clearly she is." Brent waved a nonchalant hand at her. "Walking, talking, alive." His tone was glacial, devoid of any hint of past affection.

Melanie couldn't believe she had almost slept with him. She took off her sunglasses and stared at him in disbelief. "A man tried to kill me and nearly succeeded."

He leaned toward her, taking a good look at her face. "I guess he did do a number on you. I can see a black eye poking through your makeup, and bruises on your neck, too. *Sheesh.* Did he choke you?" He reached for her.

She jerked away from his touch. The bruising on her face and neck was horrible, but at least it looked worse than it felt today. She'd done her best to hide it. Only so much makeup could do.

Waylon put up his palm, close to Brent's chest. "Watch your hands and keep them to yourself." His voice was calm, perfectly civilized, but something dangerous flickered in his eyes.

"And your name, buddy?"

"Detective Waylon Wright."

"Why is Drake Colter free?" she asked, trying to get the discussion back on track. "And don't brush it off by telling me it's complicated."

"But it is. And it isn't." Brent took a long drag on his cigarette and blew the smoke out off to the side.

She'd never been a fan of the smell of cigarettes, but after the assault last night, the scent of menthol turned her stomach.

"No lawyer doublespeak," Waylon said. "Just answer the question."

"Where to begin?" Brent asked, his tone flippant.

Waylon nudged his cowboy hat up with his knuckle. "Try the beginning."

"We believe the Sand Angel Killer first started taking victims in New Mexico, though we couldn't prove that," Brent said, "and suspected he worked his way up here to Denver."

"That's where he made his mistake and left behind DNA," Melanie said, filling in the blanks for Waylon. "When we finally tracked him down, turns out he was already in prison in Las Cruces for vandalizing the White Sands National Park, serving a one-year sentence. And we did eventually find a body out there, too, but we couldn't tie him to the murder. His incarceration made the process easy. We brought him to Denver, had him arraigned on murder charges, and he was returned to New Mexico on a court order until the trial started, where we got a conviction."

"Exactly." Brent put the cigarette in the smoking receptacle and took out another one. "There's the crux of the problem," he said as though that had explained anything.

"Yeah, that's clear as mud." Waylon waved at the air in front of him. "Would you mind?" he asked, indicating the cigarette. "Secondhand smoke kills."

"I didn't invite you to come out here and interrupt the one moment of peace that I've had today. Leave for all I care." Brent lit the cigarette. "I'm in crisis mode here."

"Focus, Brent." She snapped her fingers. "Why is that murderer on the loose?"

"Colter's appellate lawyer filed a motion to vacate the murder conviction based on a violation of the interstate agreement law approved by Congress back in 1970. The judge stated in her decision that county officials here violated the federal Interstate Agreement on Detainer's Law, or IAD, when we sent him back to prison in New Mexico as he awaited trial in the Denver murder case. The harsh reality is that the administrative decision to send him back unequivocally entitled the defendant to dismissal of the murder in the first-degree indictments with prejudice under the exacting requirements of the anti-shuttling provisions of the IAD."

A dismissal with prejudice meant that Drake Colter could not be retried in the murder case. "But there was a court order to transfer him," she said.

Brent rubbed the back of his neck. "Did you ever see one?"

"No." She shook her head. "I took your word for it."

"According to a document we received, created by the sheriff's department, it indicated a court order, but turns out that it doesn't exist." Brent blew out more smoke. "The sheriff needed Colter transferred. An administrative decision based on jail population and timing. It's a traditional practice to return prisoners to their 'home' correctional facility. Apparently, this loophole has been used before, recently by a defendant in New York, to get released. Over the next few years, I'm sure others will use it, too."

Waylon swore.

"Yeah," Brent said, smoothing a hand over his slicked-back hair, "tell me about it, buddy."

The gleam of his wedding band caught her eye and the burn of old embarrassment flared in her cheeks. For years, he'd flirted with her after hours, pretending he had feelings, constantly trying to sleep with her while he had a girlfriend unbeknownst to her the entire time. Not only had he taken credit for her work, being the face of many high-profile, career-making cases that she'd built, he had also tried to turn her into the other woman.

"Look," Waylon said, "I'm not your buddy or your pal. It's Detective."

Rolling his eyes, Brent shook his head. "I don't have time for this. Since we can't keep it quiet any longer, I have a press conference in a few minutes, where I have to explain this debacle to the media and apologize alongside the sheriff. People are going to get fired over this. I'm going to lose my job."

"Melanie almost lost her life last night." Disgust tightened Waylon's voice.

"Speaking of which, did it make the local news?" Brent asked, once again with flagrant disregard for her well-being. "I just need to know if I should include you in my statement when I talk about the recent victims."

She swallowed around the lump in her throat.

Curling his fingers into a fist, Waylon stepped toward Brent, making the DA flinch. Power emanated from him. A raw, lethal kind of strength. Every time she was near Waylon, that strength enveloped her in the comfort of a warm security blanket.

Maybe it was the sheer size of him. Maybe it was the badge and gun, although she knew and worked with plenty of other cops. None of whom ever had this effect on her.

She reminded herself that security went hand in hand with dependence, and dependence on any man wasn't something she could afford.

Melanie slid between them and put a hand on Waylon's chest. "He isn't worth it." Pivoting, she looked at Mr. Despicable. "I don't want to be mentioned. But I do want to know why Colter hasn't been arrested for the recent murders."

"There's no proof he's guilty."

"The judge, the witness and the juror…" she said, "were the bodies found in the same manner as the others?"

"They were missing for about twenty-four hours before they were found. Based on time of death, they weren't killed immediately. He kept them alive for roughly twelve to sixteen hours. But the bodies were left in exactly the same manner," Brent said. "In dunes. Impressions of sand angels."

"With the word 'sinner' written beside them?"

Blowing out smoke, Brent nodded. "Yep."

"Were any of them violated?" she asked, wondering if there had been any deviation or escalation from the other murders.

"No signs of sexual assault. Blunt force trauma to the head. Cause of death asphyxia due to ligature strangulation."

They'd all been strangled, like the previous victims. "Was sand poured in their mouths and found on their eyelids?" Those details had never been released to the press during the investigation but had come out over the course of the trial.

"Yep. The murders were all the same," Brent said.

"But why isn't Colter—"

Brent threw his hands up in the air, cutting her off. "Colter has an airtight alibi for the three."

"Which is what?" Waylon asked.

"He's at a residential community corrections facility because he didn't have any place to live and requested it, claiming he was worried he'd start doing drugs and drink again. They're helping him reintegrate and transition into society."

"A halfway house?" Waylon clenched his jaw.

Anger tangled with her frustration. "He's never tested positive for drugs," she said. Despite his claims that was the reason he couldn't remember what had happened during the timeframe when one victim, where his DNA was found, had been murdered.

"I know." Brent sighed. "But the claim is working to his benefit now."

"Which facility is he in?" Waylon asked.

"Fair Chance Treatment Center. Colter was considered present and accounted for either when the victims went missing or at the time of death. Regarding Judge Babcock, his alibi covered him when she was abducted and murdered. There was no DNA found at the crime scenes to contradict that. Our hands are tied where he's concerned. This is the greatest embarrassment of my career," Brent said, reducing the murder of three innocent women to the impact on his job. He looked around them at someone.

Melanie glanced over her shoulder to see who it was.

Susan beckoned to him with an urgent wave of her hand and pointed at her watch.

"Sorry you were attacked. Glad you're fine." The words were hurried and hollow. "Even better that I don't have to mention you." Brent stamped out his cigarette. "I've got to go. Showtime." He smoothed the front of his suit, checked his reflection in the glass and made a beeline for the door. "Wish me luck."

She wished him a speedy delivery of all the karma he deserved.

"I hope the reporters tear him to pieces," Waylon said to her.

"Ditto. But that weasel has a way of slithering out of tight, tiny corners." A remarkable survival skill.

"Come on," Waylon said, putting a hand on her back.

"Where to?" She hoped he didn't want to watch the madness of the press conference.

"Fair Chance Treatment Center. To ask Colter some questions. I'd prefer it if you hung back here or at least waited in the truck and let me do it without you, but I know you're going to insist."

Melanie had confronted plenty of criminals—thieves, arsonists, gang members, mafia bosses and murderers included— but something about Drake Colter, the darkness in his eyes, always made her blood run cold.

"I need to face him, look him in the eyes." In court, she showed no mercy when she prosecuted someone, especially a murderer. Melanie had gone after him with every tool in her arsenal, showed the world what kind of monster he really was, gotten a conviction, and the highest sentence possible: life imprisonment. Now this vicious killer was free. To do it again. She was relieved she wouldn't have to see Drake Colter on her own and that Waylon would be at her side. "I can't let him think I'm afraid of him."

Even though a part of her was terrified.

Chapter Six

At the front door of the Fair Chance Treatment Center, Waylon found it locked. He pressed the bell.

"FCTC," a bright male voice said through the speaker mounted on the outside. "How can I help you?"

"I'm Detective Wright and I'm here with ADA Merritt. We have some questions for Drake Colter."

"One moment please."

Waylon took in their surroundings again. An underprivileged neighborhood in a shady part of town. The *center* was little more than a glorified house. He didn't like that the rear was adjacent to an alley that was the perfect security blind spot for someone interested in sneaking in and out with a lower risk of detection.

A white nondescript passenger van was parked in the driveway. The glimpse of her assailant's vehicle on the surveillance footage only showed a partial side profile of the front. It could've been a passenger van or cargo.

He glanced at Melanie. Pushing her sunglasses higher on the bridge of her nose, she stood rigid, her head bowed, and appeared lost in thought. That jerk, Brent Becker, had given her plenty to contemplate.

The IAD law was a gaping hole in the justice system the size of the Grand Canyon if it allowed a convicted serial killer to be free on the streets after serving only three years of a life sentence.

The front door swung open as a chime sounded. A Black man in his late fifties, possibly early sixties, with a weathered face and receding hairline greeted them. "I'm Hershel. The lead counselor." He stepped aside, letting them in. They entered a small foyer that had a rudimentary desk, a laptop that was chained to it, and a chair. "The police have already been here several times this week to speak with Mr. Colter. I'll tell you the same thing I told them, he was present and accounted for during the times they specified."

"You saw him personally?" Melanie asked, keeping her sunglasses on inside the center.

"No. The night shift counselor does a room check at ten and another one randomly in the night and then a last one at six in the morning."

Depending on when the random check occurred, there could have been plenty of time to sneak out, commit murder, and make it back for the final inspection.

Waylon took out a pad and pen. "What's the name and number of the other counselor?"

"Kurt Parrish was on duty those three nights." Hershel rattled off his cell phone number. "He works from eight at night to eight in the morning."

"Is it possible for someone to sneak out during the night?" Melanie asked.

"Not without us knowing it." Hershel shoved his hands in the front pockets of his jeans. "When the security system isn't fully activated, like it is now, it's set to chime whenever any exterior door or window is opened. There's an electronic record. After 10:00 p.m., the security system is set. At that point, if a door or window is opened, it triggers the alarm."

"Could someone open a window at the same time a door is opened, so there's only one chime?" Mel asked.

"Sure, I suppose so." Hershel nodded. "But the security

system won't fully activate if a door or window is left open. We'd get an error."

Waylon eyed the outdated panel near the door. "Ever have any problems with the system?"

"On occasion, sure we do." Hershel gave a one-shoulder shrug. "The system is old. When a battery needs to be changed in a sensor, it doesn't work properly until the security company can come out to fix it, which can take a few days, and sometimes the plug to the hub comes loose. Takes a good five minutes to reboot."

All weaknesses in the security system that could be exploited to tamper with the electronic record.

"Any of those issues occur recently, say over the past ten days since Colter has been here?" Waylon asked.

"As a matter of fact, yes. Kurt has mentioned a few things, but nothing out of the ordinary. I'm sure it's just a coincidence. Like I said, the system is old."

The security system was ancient, but Waylon didn't believe in coincidence. Gritting his teeth, he exchanged a frustrated glance with Mel. "Do you happen to know where Mr. Colter was last night," he said, "between seven and ten?"

"Last night?" Hershel tilted his head to the side. "Was someone else killed?"

Melanie's lips flattened into a grim line. "No, sir, but I was attacked."

"Brutally," Waylon added.

"Oh my goodness. I'm so sorry to hear that." Hershel looked and sounded sincere, unlike Brent, whose callousness had been mindboggling for a human with a beating heart. "Such a shame what happened to you, but it couldn't have been Drake."

"How are you so sure?" Melanie asked.

"We usually have an hour of group therapy at six on Thursday nights, but I left early."

"How early?" Waylon interrupted. "And why did you leave?"

"It was around five or five thirty. That's when Kurt showed up early to cover the shift. Something I ate didn't agree with me or it was a twenty-four-hour bug. A few guys weren't feeling well. This morning, Kurt told me that everything was quiet. Some went to bed sick while everyone else gathered in the living room and watched the *Real Housewives* at nine, like always. A lot of the guys get into it in prison. No one ever misses an episode in this house. Unless they're feeling under the weather. The guys were all in their bedrooms at ten."

Melanie folded her arms. "Was Colter unwell last night?"

"Yes, he was. Turned into bed long before I left. Maybe around four."

"Does he share a room?" Waylon asked.

"The guys are lucky. They each have their own room. But Kurt logged them all present and accounted for at ten, at three, and again at six. I checked the logs as soon as I got in like usual. Drake was here last night."

What if the night shift guy, Kurt, had grown complacent with his job and only done a rudimentary check from the doorway? Someone claiming to be sick, or wanting to give the perception they're asleep, could stuff a few pillows in the bed to make it look like a person was there. Pretend to go to sleep early. Sneak out before the security system was fully activated.

If Colter went to his room at four, that would've given him time to drive up to Laramie, wait two hours, attack her, then return to Denver and slip back inside FCTC.

Also, within the realm of possibility that Kurt was incentivized to look the other way through bribery or intimidation.

None of this gave Waylon a warm and fuzzy feeling that Drake Colter's alibi was airtight or that the convicted killer was innocent of these recent murders and the attack on Melanie.

"You heard Hersh. I didn't do whatever you're here to ask about," another man said, waltzing into the foyer.

Drake Colter.

An average-looking guy, both in height and girth. Waylon guessed him to be around his own age, midthirties. Wearing a wife-beater, arms covered in tattoos, with rattlesnake-mean eyes and greasy blond hair, he could come across as menacing.

Dangerous. Going up against the right person.

But Waylon was *waaaay* the hell more dangerous if it came to protecting Melanie.

Colter eyed him up and down, measuring his worth. His mouth twitched, his eyes shifting away. The evil scumbag didn't want a piece of him, but the guy dared to turn his attention to Melanie.

"Hey, you look at me and speak to me," Waylon said. "Not her."

"Or else what?" Colter asked, jutting his chin up in the air.

Waylon stepped in front of her, positioning himself as a barrier and smiled. "You *do not* want to test me."

Colter took a tentative step back. "I didn't catch your name."

"Detective Waylon Wright."

"I was here last night, Detective. Hersh confirmed it and so will Kurt Parrish. Because it's the truth. So, I didn't do whatever you came here to grill me about." Colter spoke while waving his hands around in an animated manner. "I'm sick of this harassment. My sentence was vacated. Not my fault you bozos messed up, but I know my rights and I don't have to talk to you." The wretch pointed a finger in Waylon's face. "Not without my lawyer present."

Waylon glanced down at the index finger inches from his nose and resisted the urge to snatch it and snap it. But his gaze fell to the underside of Colter's forearm.

To a list tattooed on his skin in black ink.

Waylon took the man's wrist and turned it so he could read the words clearly:

Alicia Babcock
Regina Sweeney
Georgia Jenkins
Kristin Loeb
Emilio Vasquez
Melanie Merritt

"What is this?" Waylon asked. "Some kind of hit list?" Anger simmered and smoldered in his chest.

Mel stepped around to see it, along with Hershel, who peered over her shoulder.

Colter jerked his arm away from Waylon's grip and proudly held it out for them to all see. "No, it's not a hit list," he said with a maniacal grin. "Just a permanent reminder of the people responsible for trying to lock me away forever." He clasped his hands together and rubbed his palms. "But no hard feelings anymore. I'm free while you all have egg on your face. At least, the ones still breathing." His gaze cut to Melanie. "For now."

Waylon stepped in his line of sight, barely containing his fury over the not-so-veiled threat. "What do you mean by *for now*? Do you have plans for the other three on your list of targets?"

"Targets?" Colter feigned a baffled expression. "I don't have any targets, Detective. I'm not some murderous mastermind. My only plan is to abide by the house rules and focus on my reintegration into the community so that I can be a productive member of society." A smile spread on his face, a sick gleam in his eyes. "Now, if you'll excuse me. We recorded the DA's press conference earlier. I think I'll watch it again. Hope the DA and sheriff are fired before they have a chance to quit." Colter turned and walked away.

"You don't blame DA Becker for your indictment and incarceration?" Waylon asked, the question stopping the serial killer in his tracks.

"No, I don't," Colter said with his back to them. "He wasn't the one who hired that intrusive investigator, Vasquez. Encouraged the podcaster, Loeb, to have me tried in the court of public opinion. He wasn't the one who prosecuted me. Picked the jury. Gave such a heartrending closing argument. Persuaded the families of the victims to speak at my sentencing." Colter looked over his shoulder at Melanie. "I told you I was innocent. Maybe you should've listened to me. How else can you explain what's happening now?" His grin deepened, turning sinister. "Hope to see you again ADA Merritt. Next time, come back without the big fella. Maybe I'll help you before it's too late."

"Where she goes, I go." Waylon stepped over, blocking Colter's view of her again. "Look at me. Speak to me."

"Aww, is ADA Merritt someone special to you, Detective Wright? Is it true love or true lust?"

"I'll be the one asking the questions."

"Well, I still have a couple more for you. Are you a tough guy, huh? Think you're an immovable object?" Colter chuckled. "When an unstoppable force with infinite torque meets a so-called immovable object, like yourself, there's only one outcome. That object gets moved. You see, the flaw for the object is that it lacks any force holding it in place. Maybe what's coming for her can't be stopped. Not even by you."

"We'll see about that," Waylon said, anger bleeding into his voice. "I'm not going to let anything happen to her."

"You can try. Give it your best shot. But I'm willing to venture a guess that you'll fail." A smug grin tugged at his ugly mouth. He turned around, putting his back to them, and started to walk away as he whistled a tune. The melody of a nursery rhyme. "There Was An Old Lady Who Swallowed A Fly." Right before he disappeared down the hall, he said, "You better hurry back to see me. Tick tock, Ms. Melanie Merritt."

Chapter Seven

Behind the wheel of his truck, Waylon looked over at Melanie as she hung up her cell. "Emilio isn't picking up. His phone goes straight to voicemail."

"Do you still have any friends over at the Denver PD?"

"I might have a couple left."

"Good. Reach out to them. Tell them about Colter's list, your attack, and the danger that Vasquez and Loeb are in. They also need to put a cop on the halfway house at night. We need to know for certain if Colter is sneaking out."

"You don't believe Hershel? Seemed trustworthy to me."

"Maybe he doesn't have all the facts and believes what he's been told by the night shift guy. We need to question Kurt Parrish. Face-to-face. If he doesn't return my call, we'll have to swing back by the Fair Chance Treatment Center while he's on duty."

Melanie's phone chimed. "It's a text from Kristin Loeb. She's meeting with the Sand Angelites right now and can't talk. She feels like she's on the verge of getting some kind of a lead."

"Angelites? Care to elaborate?"

She took a deep breath. "We tried to label Colter the Sand Dune Killer. One of the detectives working on the case mentioned the impression of an angel the murderer made with the victims. The media dubbed him the Sand Angel Killer instead and it stuck. Guess it sold more papers and got more clicks online. The Angelites are a bunch of Colter's groupies. They formed a cult. Idolize him. They all wear gypsum around their necks. A soft, pale blue crystal that's supposed to symbolize soothing and peaceful energy. Another name for the stone happens to be Angelite."

"A cult for a serial murderer?"

"Happened with Manson. A lot of sick people out there. But the Sand Angelites claim that he's different because he only went after *sinners*," she said, using air quotes. "They believe he is cleansing the world of evil. How is that for twisted logic?" She sighed. "Though I can't fathom what any of his victims were guilty of besides the fact they were women. Vulnerable at the right place and right time for him to strike."

"What else does her text say?"

Melanie looked back at the phone. "Kristin is here in Denver up from Pagosa Springs. She's staying at the Mile-High City Motel and will be back to her room later tonight. She's willing to meet and share what she learns if we want to hang around."

"Yeah. We can stay the night at the same place. Chat with her and make sure she stays safe."

"You need to make a U-turn. The motel is in the opposite direction." Staring at the phone, Mel smiled. "She recommends the tavern across the street for dinner."

"Sounds like a plan. Tell me more about her."

"Kristin is an investigative journalist and true crime podcaster. One of the victims of the Sand Angel Killer was a student at her alma mater, the University of Denver. That's when she took an interest. She sheds light on unsolved murders, missing persons in settings that one might otherwise associate with a quaint getaway. The sand dune murders were perfect for her. Once we met, we clicked. She's warm and funny, has this way of disarming people."

"That's probably why she's so successful." His cell phone

rang. "It's the night shift guy." He put the call on speaker through Bluetooth. "You've reached Detective Wright."

"Hi. This is Kurt Parrish. I got your messages. Sorry. I was sleeping. What's this about? I already spoke with some of your friends at the Denver Police Department."

"I'm from the Laramie PD."

"Oh, um, I didn't realize. You're a long way from home and I believe outside your jurisdiction."

Not easily sidetracked, Waylon said, "I had a few questions that I'd like to ask you in person if you don't mind."

Silence.

"Mr. Parrish? Are you still there?"

"Uh, actually, I do mind. I've been cooperative. You can get copies of my statements from the cops here."

"This is involving an assault that occurred last night," Waylon said, "while you were on duty. Do you have ten minutes for a face to face?"

A beat of hesitation. "Is this about Drake Colter?"

"It is."

"He was present and accounted for. In bed all night. He was sick. Ate something bad."

"Then it'll only take two minutes instead of ten, sir. We can stop by your home now if you'll give me the address."

"I don't have anything else to add," Kurt Parrish said. "Sorry I can't be more helpful. I, um, I hope that's enough for you. Got to go. I've got something important to do, an appointment I need to get to before work. I need to go." The call disconnected.

Mel raised an eyebrow. "Kurt Parrish sounded nervous."

"I agree. Cops tend to make suspects nervous. Not innocent people who are being asked rudimentary questions unless they have something to hide."

"That's not always true. A lot of people in the inner city are suspicious of the police. When I lived here, I was an advocate of the Denver PD community outreach program, to foster communication, address concerns, and build trust."

Back home, the cops were the good guys, pillars of the community, to be trusted. In most cases. The Laramie PD did have a problem with corrupt officers until the chief cleaned it up. Problems like that were probably more widespread in places like Denver. Not that he'd had much inner-city experience.

"We need to figure out what's making Parrish nervous," he said. "See if he knows more. Since we're spending the night, I say we go back to FCTC first thing in the morning when his guard is down and he thinks we've moved on."

"That strategy could work. I should call the office and check in with Darcy. She told me Gordon was out unexpectedly today. It's been happening a lot lately and I've had to pick up the slack. Since I'm not there, I just want to make sure everything is running smoothly."

While she spoke to the paralegal, Melanie finished giving him directions to the motel. Down the street on the corner was a large pharmacy store where they grabbed toiletries and a few essentials since they hadn't planned to stay the night.

He parked at the Mile-High City Motel and got them a room. First floor. Room 120—dingy carpet, outdated décor, musty smell. Typical low-budget place.

Across the street, the hostess at the tavern seated them at a booth in a secluded area, at Melanie's request, so they could speak privately. They ordered, got their drinks and waited for their meals.

"I'm sure today was a shock for you," he said. "Finding out about the three latest murders."

"That's an understatement. I'm on a hit list." She took a sip of her margarita on the rocks, no salt on the rim. "I think what's more disconcerting is that the DA's office here neglected to notify me. If they'd only given me the common-sense courtesy of a heads-up, I never would've left work late on my own."

Brent's carelessness made Waylon want to rearrange the DA's face. One phone call from Brent and Mel would've had a sheriff's deputy escort her to her vehicle.

But maybe it would have been worse if her assailant had seen the deputy and altered his plans. Decided to wait until she was home. Alone. Asleep. Even more vulnerable.

They needed to determine if Colter was behind this latest string of murders or if it was someone else, and stop him. Fast. "Colter claims he wasn't the Sand Angel Killer. Is it possible you got the wrong guy?"

"His DNA was found on two victims. We confirmed he was in Colorado on the dates of the murders, which contradicted the statement of his alibi. Georgia Jenkins, his girlfriend. Her statement fell apart under scrutiny. She claimed Colter threatened her, forced her to lie to the authorities."

"Any evidence to suggest that it might have been two perps working together?"

"None."

Their food was brought to the table. He cut into his steak while Melanie picked at her pasta. She'd barely eaten all day, though he understood her loss of appetite. After the last twenty-two hours, no wonder food held little appeal for her.

"Any differences between the murders in New Mexico and Colorado?" he asked.

"In New Mexico, it looked like he was just getting started. The same blunt force trauma to the head and strangulation, with the bodies found in sand dunes." She tossed back a swallow of her margarita. "But the ones in Colorado had more flourish to them. The impressions of the sand angels with the bodies of the victims carefully placed in the center. *Sinner* scrolled in the sand. Evolution and escalation are typical in serial killers."

"Do you think Colter attacked you? Snuck out somehow? Or that it was someone else working on his behalf?" Either way, he felt certain that sick murderer was responsible.

"I wish I knew for sure. My gut tells me that he's getting help of some kind, if only we could pin down to what degree. Maybe it's from Kurt Parrish. The alibi is strong and apparently enough to dissuade the police from digging too much deeper into Colter."

"Did you hear back from your friends in the Denver PD?"

"I did. There's already a request to have Drake Colter officially monitored. One detective I know well has been watching the house at night after the second murder, but they need additional personnel because the back of the center abuts an alley. They don't have eyes on it. If he did sneak out last night, he used the alley and wasn't seen." She ran distressed fingers through her hair.

For a moment, he was mesmerized by the way the strands moved like a shimmery curtain of dark water, rich black and so thick. She was the most beautiful thing on the face of the planet.

He lowered his head. "You got a speedy response." Meant she still had a good working relationship with law enforcement. "So, tell me, what were your reasons for leaving Denver? Did one of them have something to do with Brent? I take it that he was the ex who was happy you left?"

She finished her margarita and caught the attention of the waiter. "I'm going to need another."

With a nod, the server took the empty glass.

"You asked if the relationship ended badly," she continued, "but you didn't ask the nature of that relationship. He was my boss. There was heavy flirtation on his part. Only after business hours when we worked late. Outside of the office at conferences, work dinners, that sort of thing."

"Did you ever sleep with him?" He hoped the answer was

no. A slimeball such as Brent didn't deserve to be with a woman like Mel.

"I considered it."

His gut clenched. "Why?"

She hesitated. "I get lonely and I have needs."

Easy enough to find someone to scratch an itch. No need for her to settle for the likes of Becker.

"But I only entertained the thought," she said. "The flirting was one-sided on his part."

"You're beautiful. You could have any guy you want." She was the woman he should not have been able to get. Only by luck, or fate, that she'd gone to Crazy Eddie's that night, where she'd had her choice of cowboys, and picked him.

Smiling, she shook her head. "I'm also direct, blunt and assertive," she said, forgetting to list unapologetic about what she wanted—an admirable trait. "Plenty of guys find that off-putting."

Their server delivered her drink and hurried off to another table.

"When I lived here in Denver," she continued, "I worked long hours. Brent was interested and convenient."

"But he's such a—"

"I know," she cut him off, stopping the crass word from leaving his lips. "Nothing about him spelled *good guy*. That was part of his limited appeal. It meant I'd never fall in love with him." Mel stabbed a piece of penne with her fork. "The upside of his cold personality was that everything would've stayed all business at work. Outside of the office, things would've been casual. But it also would've been a human resources disaster waiting to happen. When I make DA, I don't want anyone to think I slept my way to the top."

Relief seeped through him, but one thing niggled at him. "Brent's appeal was that you'd never fall in love. You don't want that? Love. Marriage."

Her brow crinkled, caution darkening her eyes. "Sex is simple. Love is complicated. Difficult to balance with a demanding job. You know how many detectives end up getting divorced?"

"A lot." The divorce rate for cops was like seventy-five percent. "But you didn't answer my question about love and marriage."

She flicked a glance at her drink and then back at him. "Only a fool would want to fall in love with their boss. Besides, any distraction would hinder me from making DA. Not help me."

Carefully chosen words. Still not an answer. "Or it could be nice to have someone in your corner, no matter what."

Not meeting his eyes, she pushed pasta around on her plate with her fork.

A chime had her grabbing her phone. "It's Kristin. The text says she's onto something big. Will be back after eleven tonight. Room 204. She'll call once she gets in and compiles her notes about the Savior connection."

"Savior?"

"Savior with a capital S." She held up her phone, turning the screen toward him.

That gave them several hours until they could learn more from Loeb.

"Hey," he said. "Your career aside, I'm glad you didn't sleep with Brent. I don't like thinking about you with him." Or any other man for that matter.

"Is that why you wanted to hit him earlier?"

"Partly. But mostly the callous narcissist just had it coming," he said; and she grinned at him—a slow, devastating smile that sent a ripple of heat through him. "If you two didn't hook up, then why did the work relationship end badly?" He wondered.

"Four years of overtures, including the night before my last day. He stopped by my house and laid it on thick, but I had zero interest. He said rude things. Called me an iceberg. Assumed sex with me would've been like sleeping with a dead fish."

Ouch. Little did Becker know that though Mel was tough and remained levelheaded at work, she was passionate about everything. Once you got past her defenses, she was affectionate and open, the warmest, most vivacious person.

"The next day at the office, when I was saying my goodbyes, he announced that he was engaged."

Waylon set his fork down. "I take it you didn't know he was seeing anyone."

"Didn't have a clue. His girlfriend never attended work functions. I later learned because she travels a lot. He never mentioned he was involved with anyone, but I hadn't asked either," she said, her voice low, and the interrogation she had put him through when they'd met in the honky-tonk suddenly made sense. "One thing for him to take credit for my work. Quite another to try to use me as a side piece. Cheating is the worst kind of deception. Robs a person of their pride. Violates trust. I wasn't his girlfriend, but it was still humiliating." She shook her head and he wanted to erase the hurt look from her eyes and punch Brent in the face. "My dad cheated on my mother."

"I'm surprised, based on the way you talk about them. They seem like soulmates."

"They are. I meant my biological father, Aadesh. Not Frederick, who raised me as his own. I consider him my dad. My mom's first husband hurt her deeply. She couldn't forgive him. He left, remarried, and never looked back. He's a lawyer, too. Coincidentally." Her voice lowered. "Sometimes when I disconnect and put messy emotions in neat boxes, she says I'm like him. Aadesh. A chip off the old block." Her pained expression made him reach for her hand, but she pulled it away into her lap. "I may be like him in some ways, but I wouldn't cheat. Not ever."

"I know you wouldn't." He let Melanie absorb that, his trust and faith in her.

"Thank you."

"For the record, I would never cheat either. Who we are isn't all about genetics. I told you my father was mean-spirited."

"Disrespectful to your mom. I figured that's why you go out of your way to be so polite."

"It was more than that. He was abusive. Until I got big enough to stop him. That's when we moved from Wayward Bluffs to Bison Ridge." Later his mother remarried and moved his siblings farther north in Wyoming while he joined the army. After serving, he'd missed Wayward Bluffs and bought a house there. "My father is the reason I'm so careful with the way I deal with people, how I present myself. I never want to scare a woman, kids, hurt anyone, because I lose control. My worst fear is becoming my father."

"You never would. Never could."

He appreciated hearing that. Needed to know she believed in him. "I used to be afraid of my anger when I was younger. Shoved all that rage and confusion behind a door. Bolted it firmly. But the army taught me I had to let it out. To be a good ranger. To live." Also, to love. "Anger isn't bad if you control it, learn how to channel it to achieve an objective." The six years he'd served, becoming a ranger, had helped make him the man he was today.

"You're one of the good ones. Like my dad, Frederick. The opposite of your father and the Brent Beckers of the world." She sipped her second margarita. "Can you believe Brent had the nerve to email me an informal invitation to his wedding?"

"After meeting that pompous jerk, I can. But the way he treated you back then and earlier today says a lot more about him and his character than it does about you." Melanie was exceptional in so many ways and it was Brent's loss for not seeing it. Waylon restrained a sigh, wishing it was at least his gain. "Besides the bonehead Brent, what was the other reason that made you leave Denver?" He finished his cola.

"In a nutshell, I was being stalked."

He nearly choked on the soda sliding down his throat. "What? Why didn't you tell me?"

"Once I left Colorado, it stopped." Her tone was casual, her demeanor nonchalant. "There was no reason to mention it to you or anyone else when we met."

"You should've told me and Holden last night. It might be relevant. Couldn't you have gotten a restraining order against the guy?"

"If it had only been one person, sure, but it was tough to get a restraining order against multiple people. Just when I thought I knew who they all were, more emerged, like cockroaches from the dark. Easier to simply leave."

An ex or a rebuffed admirer sure, but… "Multiple people?" This was starting to sound like the strangest stalking case he'd ever heard of.

"The Sand Angelites. They made me their pet project. Everywhere I went, one or more of them followed. They would pour a circle of sand around my car, sometimes leaving a bag of it near my front door. At night, they would pop up at the grocery store, in the parking garage, if I went to a restaurant, outside my house but across the street, always holding lit blue candles. Standing there, silent, staring, pointing at me. It would creep me out. But since it was in public and they never threatened me—"

"The cops couldn't do anything about those incidents," he said, finishing her sentence.

She nodded. "The last straw was when one of them broke into my home, cut himself, smeared his blood on the walls and threw sand everywhere. Isaac Meacham. I found him sitting in my living room, cross-legged, holding one of those damn blue candles. That was it for me. I gave notice at my job, sold my place, packed my bags and got out of there."

Not like Melanie to tuck her tail and run. She was a fighter. Especially when angered. Those Colter groupies must've really gotten to her.

Under the table, Waylon clenched his hand against the urge to touch her, comfort her. He hated how those people had terrorized her. "I take it you had him arrested."

"Of course. But I stopped sleeping and eating, and started wondering what would happen next." She chuckled, the sound cheerless, her face grim. "Out of all the big cases Brent stole and took to trial himself, I don't know why he didn't take that one off my hands. The one favor he could've done for me and didn't. Those Angelites made my life a living hell for months."

"Maybe the Sand Angelites are the ones who have evolved and are escalating things. And if they are, then Kristin isn't safe around them."

"They've proven themselves to be creeps. Not killers. And Kristin is used to poking the bear, so to speak. No warning is going to stop her from taking risks."

"Poke enough bears and eventually you get mauled." He'd done enough poking as a detective to know.

Their server stopped at the table. "Can I get you two anything else?"

Melanie tapped her half-full glass. "Another margarita."

"Also, the bill and a to-go box for her," Waylon said.

Melanie didn't consume alcohol often, but when she did, she could hold her own for a woman with such a small frame. Still, he figured three margaritas should be her max since he wanted her to be lucid and able to think clearly when they got back to the room.

"No problem," the waiter said and left.

"The odds are someone is helping Colter," Waylon said. "Makes sense for it to be his groupies."

Tipping her head to the side, she pursed her lips. "Let's say it is them, doing his bidding in regard to the murders. One thing I can't wrap my head around is why would they wait until Drake Colter is released? Why not go after the people responsible for putting him in jail a year ago, two, three, when he was first convicted? Why would they deliberately implicate a man they idolize and potentially jeopardize his newfound freedom?"

Those were big questions they needed to answer.

Once they did, they'd be one step closer to catching a killer.

Chapter Eight

Three margaritas later, with Melanie putting most of her food in a to-go container, they paid the bill and left the tavern. The day had been long, draining, riddled with disastrous surprises. She needed to decompress and reset.

The only problem was her preferred method involved Waylon.

Naked. In bed.

With him, she'd made the mistake of breaking all her rules. No last names. No spending the night. No getting personal. No emotional investment.

Months of strictly sex between them had blurred together and soon she had been spending more nights with him than apart. Disentangling from him in the morning with nothing but coffee in her belly and an ache in her chest. After a year or two that had blossomed into weekends. Meals in bed. Dancing in that honky-tonk, Crazy Eddie's. Deep conversations after making love where she found it hard *not* to share. He'd not only slipped into her bed but also past her defenses, carving his way into her heart without her realizing until it was too late.

As they crossed the tavern's parking lot, she glanced over at him. Strong. Ruggedly handsome. Unequivocally hot.

Melanie wanted to feel him, skin to skin, that fierce pleasure only he could give her. But the idea of crossing the newly established line would be selfish and needy.

They walked to the corner and waited for the traffic light

to change. He took her hand in his as they crossed the street. Smooth. Natural. Holding his hand was unexpectedly nice. His calluses rubbed against her skin and she liked the feel of his fingers, of him touching her, even in this small way.

Everything about Waylon, from the strength of his body to his work-worn hands, to the knife in his boot, to his protective instincts, and that compelling confidence, made it evident he was as fundamental as a cowboy could get.

And every bit as appealing.

Outside their room, Waylon wrapped a powerful arm around her waist and, spinning her back to the door, pressed his body to hers.

She put a palm to his cheek. Traced the line of the scar under his eye. Raked her gaze over the others—one bisecting his left eyebrow, a ridge on his forehead, another near his right cheekbone and on his chin. Wounds he'd gotten in a fight with Montgomery Powell when they'd been hotheaded teens. Waylon had been pushed into a trophy case and the broken glass had sliced up his face.

Now, the scars were faint, not grisly, giving him a rugged allure. Proof of his strength and good character. No matter the pain he'd suffered, the teasing he'd endured with mean kids calling him Scarface, despite the violence of his father, going to war in the army, he was a gentle, beautiful soul.

And sexy as sin.

Without a word of warning, he leaned in and captured her mouth in a hard, quick kiss that left her lips tingling and her thoughts scattered. The thrill of it shot straight down to her core. He tasted so good, the scent of him so *masculine*.

Her heart thundered, beating like a drum, and she wondered if he felt it against his chest.

She met his gaze, his warm eyes slowly softening her body and her resolve. "We talked about this." Months ago. On Christmas morning no less. After he'd shocked her with tickets for a romantic getaway. Instead of saying *yes* or giving him a gift wrapped with a red bow in return, she'd broken his heart.

"Did we?" His voice was husky and full of gravelly heat.

"Yes, and we already said everything we needed to." The boundaries had been clearly redrawn and now she wanted to erase them. But she didn't want to toy with his heart.

"As I recall, we didn't even come close." A hint of a grin danced on his lips. "You talked and I listened. To a lawyer, that might seem like a conversation. But to a cowboy, that's called a speech." The corners of his mouth hitched higher into an enigmatic smile, like he was hiding something, tempting her to peel off his clothes and figure out what it was. He gently slid the rough pads of his fingers over her cheek, his thumb stroking her bottom lip, sending a visceral ache that punched low and heavy, expanding fast and deep through muscle and bone and blood.

His gaze dropped to her mouth.

Her breath caught in her throat as the air around them stilled. A flash fire started low in her belly, but in the center of her chest was a corkscrew twist of emotion.

This here, with him, was something more. Stronger. Deeper. Scarier.

"I don't want to hurt you." When she'd told him she'd wanted space, that they needed to take an indefinite break, it had gutted her. She couldn't bear to put either of them through that again. "I don't want to cause you any more pain."

"Then don't." Leaning down, he breathed into her ear, "I can help you relax for a little bit. Give you what you need."

A shiver ran through her from her scalp to the space between her toes. If anybody could give her what she needed, this man could. He knew how to touch her, kiss her, hold her, when to talk dirty, when to be sweet. When to be rough and when to be tender.

Her thighs tingled, and she moistened her lips, debating. "You'd regret it."

"Never. I'll never regret a single moment with you." The glint of certainty in his eyes sucker-punched her heart. "Not even the ones that wound me."

It was suddenly hard for her to breathe. Where was his survival instinct when it came to her? "Why not when you should?"

"This isn't about me. It's about you. I can take your mind off things," he drawled, his voice all silky and rough at the same time. "Let me."

Melanie sure needed the escape, but as tempting as his offer was, this wasn't just one night for Waylon. He wanted more. A commitment. To go public. Marriage. A family. He wanted everything.

And she couldn't give him that. "It wouldn't be fair."

One of his big hands cupped her bottom and squeezed playfully. "Says who?"

"Me."

"All right. If it's not fair, then it's only because I have feelings you don't share." He studied her like this was some kind of test.

Her chest tightened. That couldn't be further from the truth. Her feelings for him ran deeper than he knew. She wanted him to be the one she turned to for everything, celebrate wins together, console each other through losses. Go to sleep with him, wake up beside him. She wanted to be his emergency contact, to be *his person*.

But wanting something and having it were two different things.

"It wouldn't be fair because, for me, it would only be sex." She was excellent at compartmentalization. "But for you—"

"Hold on," he said, cutting her off. "You can't speak for me, darling. Tonight, the deal is no rules. No boundaries. Forget about fair. When we make love, that kind of exchange between us doesn't get any more honest. All you have to do is take what you want." Stroking her back, his fingers playing over her spine, he looked at her, making her believe he understood everything about her.

"Waylon."

He gave her a sly grin that held way too much of a tiger's edge. Like he was on the prowl and not the one about to be used for sex.

"How about I do the taking until you tell me to stop." He claimed her mouth before she could respond, his tongue thrusting in, his other palm sliding from her waist, clasping her bottom in a two-handed grip, and grinding her closer.

Heat flamed through her body. The buzz from the margaritas mixed with the natural high Waylon always gave her had her swooning.

Maybe she could indulge and blame it on too many margaritas later.

His kiss deepened, his touch growing more urgent. Demanding.

Desire built low in her belly, coiling like a spring.

The room key jangled as he pulled it from his pocket, unlocked the door. He hauled her inside, both stumbling across the carpet.

He toed the door shut. Flipped the lock. Dropped the key. Kissed her again, clasping the back of her neck, his fingers diving in her hair. "Need you." He angled his head for a deeper fit, long sweeps of his tongue sliding over hers. Torrid, hot, edging toward desperate. Familiar heat burned between them as his other hand tunneled under her shirt to stroke a hot path over her bare skin. "Need to be inside you."

That did it, muddling her brain and melting the last of her resistance.

Kissing him, touching him, she kept waiting for a sense of self-preservation, of warning, to kick in. For her body to stiffen, reminding her she should absolutely not do this again.

Instead, her body betrayed her, arching toward Waylon like being pulled by some magnetic force.

She tossed his hat and peeled off his blazer. The T-shirt hugged well-defined muscles and well-worn jeans molded the rest of him. Clutching his sleek, sculpted biceps, she gave a low groan.

Mine.

The terrible stray thought made her heart stutter for all it implied. Possessiveness. Weakness. But she wanted him to be hers, if only for one more night. Needed every part of him. Intended to take it, yet her mind wouldn't shut down. "This is probably a mistake—"

Silencing her with a kiss, he tossed her shirt to the floor and unhooked her lace bra. "I am not a mistake."

She cringed on the inside, her eyes widening, mouth going dry. Being careful with her words, cautious with the hearts of previous lovers, had never been a concern. But Waylon was different.

"I didn't mean you," she said, putting her hand to his cheek.

"Good." He scooped her up like she weighed nothing at all, carried her to the bed and laid her crossways.

Then he climbed on top of her, the solid steel of his powerful arms braced on either side of her shoulders. All that warm muscle and delicious strength pressed against her much smaller figure. Waylon made her feel tiny, dainty. She loved the sexy contrast.

His gaze sharpened. "Stop thinking and relax." Smiling, he palmed her B-cup breast, his large hand almost enveloping her.

She shivered beneath his touch, giddy with anticipation. "Is that an order?" She ran her fingers through his thick hair, bringing his face closer until their lips were a hairsbreadth apart.

"Considering the only time that you follow them is in bed,

yes." He nipped her bottom lip and kissed her, this time harder, slower. Deeper. Longer. "The first of many more tonight."

He was strong, insistent. Not the kind of man who'd treat her delicately, like she was made of porcelain. He expected and gave an uninhibited physicality. Melanie didn't have to think her way through intimacy with him. Didn't have to think at all.

Only feel. Enjoy.

She unfastened his belt buckle and lowered his zipper. "I'm all yours. Ready to please. Ready to be pleased."

He chuckled, a rich, melodic rumble that sent a bolt of wet heat between her thighs. Lifting up, he peeled her pants and underwear off. "Spread your legs." He spoke with that commanding tone she loved in the bedroom, and she did as he demanded, gladly, eagerly.

He settled between her thighs and every nerve ending in her body sparked to life.

There was lust and then there was *this*.

Need and desire and…*love*, inextricably tied together.

She slipped her hand into his boxer briefs, closing her palm around him. He gave a ragged groan, his hips flexing so that his hardness moved against her. The heady masculine scent of him sank deep into her pores. He nibbled her earlobe and trailed his mouth along the side of her neck, his warm breath making her toes curl with want.

"I've missed this," he said, capturing her wrists in one hand and pinning them above her head. His other hand slid from her breast, across her stomach, to the apex of her thighs, and she sighed at the blazing contact of his fingers, at the liquid pleasure that ran through her, arching beneath him. "Missed you."

Me, too. During their time apart, she'd grown numb, doing her best to deny the ache of loneliness.

He slid down her body until his head was between her legs and then his mouth on her, his palms on her thighs, anchoring her in place.

She gasped, now at his mercy. "Oh… *Waylon*." The choke-hold of desire tightening into unbearable need made her catch back a sob. The craving for him was primal. She no longer cared about the consequences. Only wanted this. That rush from the feel of him. Waylon's mouth. His hands. His hips rolling against hers, taking her to the edge.

She whimpered, trying to hold on, not wanting to lose herself completely yet. "Wait."

"Done waiting."

Smiling, she cupped his face and tugged him up. "I want you with me."

He crawled over her again, grabbed his wallet and pulled out a condom. "This thing is ancient. Do I need it?"

They hadn't used one in two years when they'd decided unofficially to be exclusive. She hadn't been with anyone else and since he was still carrying around the same old one, she figured neither had he.

"No, you don't." She shoved the rest of his clothes down off him.

Closing her eyes, she arched her hips up to meet him as he glided in. She gasped at the sweet force of it. Her body clenched, nerves thrumming with the searing pleasure of being joined.

She and Waylon had right now.

And now had to be enough. So, she did the only thing she could. Kissed him. Held him. Laid herself bare.

For tonight.

Chapter Nine

Waylon held Melanie in his arms. Here with him, he could keep her safe.

Her head was on his chest, her arm draped across his stomach. They were sweaty and sated. Curled close around one another.

The only thing that had mattered when he made love to her was *her* pleasure, *her* well-being.

Not that it hadn't been easy for him to enjoy himself, too. Everything about Melanie spiked his hunger. Outside of bed, her bossiness was an odd kind of turn-on. In bed, her submission, her eagerness, even hotter.

Making love to her after so long undid him. Stripped him down to the marrow. Being with her again reinforced everything he felt for her. He'd do whatever it took to protect her.

This wasn't just a job, and she was more than someone he had to protect. She was everything to him, the one person on the planet who mattered most.

Waylon trailed a finger over the rise of her shoulder, down the deep dip of her waist and over the delicate curve of her hip. "I want you," he whispered, his lips against her hair.

She nuzzled her nose along the side of his neck, sliding her leg between his thighs. "You just had me, cowboy."

"From the second you walked into Crazy Eddie's, and I saw you, it's only been you." Since their breakup, he'd managed a few dates. Nothing had made him want a second. Never any desire to sleep with other women. None had compared to Melanie. Deep down, he'd held out hope she'd come back to him. Waylon rolled on top of her, caging her with his body, because the next words out of his mouth would make her want to bolt from the bed. "When I say I want you, I mean I want us again. A real *us*."

Mel stiffened and then pushed his arm to get up.

But he didn't budge. "Don't run from me." His voice was gentle. "Or this discussion."

"You're no longer giving me orders I'm willing to follow. Get off me. I want to shower." She pushed his chest, urging him to move away, all the while writhing naked underneath him.

A confusing contrast.

He settled more of his weight on her lower body to keep her from arousing him further. "You owe me a conversation. Please, Mel."

Squeezing her eyes shut, she threw her head back against the pillow and sighed. Seconds ticked by where the sound of her uneven breathing filled the space between them. "Okay. Fine. Let's get it over with."

He gathered his thoughts. This might be his one chance to get answers. To convince her they should be together. "When you found out I was a detective with the LPD, why didn't you end things then? Why did you continue to see me?" He'd learned she was the new ADA much earlier but hadn't mentioned it or that he was a cop. Too afraid of what might happen.

Nothing scared him, except the prospect of losing her.

"When I moved to Wyoming, I figured I'd find a lover on my terms. Picking random guys up in a bar wasn't my style. You were the first and, for nine months, what I had with you was incredible. Until one of your cases landed on my desk. I should've ended it before both our hearts got any deeper entangled. I'm sorry I didn't. All right?"

A lot of words, none of which answered his question. "Not good enough."

"Just find yourself someone normal and easy. Someone to give you babies, who'll have dinner on the table for you when you get home."

Melanie was complicated, but beautiful and brilliant. One of the toughest people he knew. Getting her to see how special she was, to fight for him rather than against him, would be an uphill battle. But he wasn't a quitter.

Not when he wanted something, and he wanted Mel in his life.

"What is normal? What would I do with a woman who's easy?" Waylon had tried to move on, to forget about her, but the love he had for her never faded. "Maybe I can be the one who has supper waiting for you. Might not be home-cooked, but I can make sure it's hot." He heaved a sigh of exasperation, realizing what she was doing. "Stop trying to sidetrack me. You thought about breaking up with me sooner, but you didn't." He'd already been a goner at that point, totally hooked, craving her when they were apart. But letting their relationship bloom for three years, only to ice him out, had devastated him. "Why not? I wasn't important to you. It was only a dalliance, right?" Waylon waited for a response. "Was it a game? The forbidden fruit tasted better, huh?" He wanted to know. Needed a straight answer. "Mel."

"I didn't mean it. I only said those things to keep Holden from looking any deeper into the mystery man who'd given me flowers. Into you." She slung her forearm over her eyes like an added layer of protection. "I didn't end things with you because…because I had already fallen for you. I liked what we had. The way you made me feel. Trust is hard for me. But

I trust you, completely. I care for you. I know it was selfish and reckless and risky, but I didn't want to lose you."

Shock rocketed through him, her admission echoing in his head.

But she'd thrown away their relationship so easily, so abruptly, that it had made his head spin. Her actions made even less sense now.

Then again, caring about someone didn't mean you loved them. "Look at me."

She hesitated.

"Look. At. Me."

Slowly, she slid her arm from her face and her gaze lifted to his. Tears welled in her eyes.

"I love you," he said, and she swallowed convulsively, going rigid underneath him. "I would've sworn you felt the same. That's why I bought those airline tickets to the Caribbean." Surprising her with them for Christmas had been a risk. One he'd been willing to take. They had spent three straight days together, making love, talking, eating, watching TV, all mostly in bed. Tim McGraw's "Shotgun Rider" had come on the radio. He'd taken it as a sign the time was right. Serenaded her, belting out the lyrics from his heart. The way she'd smiled, the light in her eyes, had made him certain they were meant to be. "I wanted to take things to the next level. Why did you push me away? And don't give me any garbage about your job."

Tears leaked from her eyes but her brow furrowed. "You thought I was lying?"

"I wanted a real relationship, for things to get serious, and it scared you. So, you ran from me." *Like a coward.* But he swallowed those words, sensing the insult would only derail them when he wanted their relationship back on track.

"Yes, it scared me. You were pushing me for everything. I didn't know how to make it work and keep it a secret. We were doomed to fail eventually anyway. But I didn't lie to you. I've never been dishonest with you about anything."

"The Wyoming Rules of Professional Conduct for attorneys prohibit sex with clients but doesn't directly address whether prosecutors may have relationships with police officers working on their cases. I looked it up."

Narrowing her eyes, she punched him in the gut, hard, and shoved his chest. "Move. Let me up right this instant, Waylon Wright."

He eased off her, crawling away.

Sitting up, she scooted back until she hit the headboard. She wiped the moisture from her eyes and glared at him. "Since I started seeing you, that very issue was raised in two different cases. One in Kentucky and the other in Illinois, in sensational fashion I might add. Both with *female* prosecutors who were romantically involved with lead detectives working on cases they took to trial. One prosecutor was suspended by her office and publicly humiliated until she quit. In the other case, a judge vacated a sentence in a notorious murder and local officials called for the prosecutor's resignation. It was stated that defendants have a right to trial by a disinterested prosecutor whose vision is not clouded and an intimate relationship between a prosecuting attorney and a lead investigator is considered anything but disinterested. An emotional entanglement could keep a prosecutor from disclosing problems in a case that might embarrass the investigator, among other things." She brought her knees into her chest and wrapped her arms around her legs. "If we continued, the way you wanted, I'd have to disclose my relationship with you and ensure all the cases you're a detective on are assigned to someone else."

Perfect. There was a way for them to be together. "That's our solution. Do that."

"How about, *I'm sorry I called you a liar, Mel*?" She hopped out of the bed and folded her arms, covering her breasts. "Or try apologizing for using sex to emotionally manipulate me."

"I'm sorry I thought you lied, but what happened between us was honest. We agreed on no rules, no boundaries tonight. I'm not sorry you open up after sex, and I'm not sorry you had three margaritas." In the afterglow, with her walls lowered, when shades of vulnerability surfaced, he felt closest to her.

Her chin tucked toward her chest. "You admit it? You hatched this plan in the restaurant."

"This is the only way you talk to me." He stood and gently clasped her shoulders. Leaning in, he put his mouth to hers in a firm, quick press of his lips. She tasted warm, but her sweetness had a bite. "You're trying to sidetrack me by picking a fight." He lowered his forehead to hers. "You just told me we can be together. No more hiding, if that's what you want. Is it?"

"There is a way, but it comes at a cost. To me. One that impacts my career and not yours." She jerked loose from his grip. "One that limits me and not you. One that exposes me to public scrutiny, as a woman, in a manner that you will never experience. Those women had their sex lives dissected in the media, with former lovers, who weren't even relevant to those cases, giving comments about them. The worst you'd endure is a bunch of high-fives from some of the guys on the force for sleeping with the ADA." She shook her head, her features twisted in misery, as though he had asked the unthinkable. "I want to be the district attorney someday. I've worked incredibly hard for it. But that won't happen if I declare to the world we've been sleeping together and have to recuse myself from your future cases. All your previous cases that I've prosecuted could be looked at and reopened. Criminals could walk free."

"You're picking your career over us?" This spark, this connection, didn't happen every day. Hell, he wanted to marry her. Spend the rest of his days with her.

"Don't you get it? I'm the one who has to choose. The one who has to sacrifice something. Not you."

"I'm not asking you to sacrifice. But I am asking, how do you feel about me? Do you love me?"

"This isn't helpful." Melanie lowered her head. "I don't want to do this."

Maybe that was his answer. Or the only one he'd get from her.

"You're a selfish coward." He spoke the words without thinking, but she needed to hear it. "I've done everything in my power to get you to fall in love with me, to fight for us. In an alternate universe, perhaps, you would." He wished she would simply tell him that she didn't love him and put him out of his misery. "But we're not in that multiverse timeline. We're in this one, where you make the rules and I just have to live with them."

Her gaze lifted to his. "That's not fair."

"Yeah, well, it's the truth."

Turning away from him, she grabbed her things. "I'm going to shower and get dressed. It's late. Kristin should be back at her room by now or sometime soon."

Melanie marched to the bathroom and slammed the door.

Dropping to the bed, Waylon scrubbed his hands over his face. Frustration welled in his chest. That conversation had not gone as he had hoped.

What bothered him the most was he'd told her he loved her. Not just tonight but also on Christmas. Flat-out asked her how she felt this time and she never said those three little words back.

He snatched his boxer briefs from the floor, put them on, grabbed his jeans and shoved his legs in. By the time the shower stopped, he was fully dressed, cowboy hat on his head. He sat on the bed, waiting for her.

The lump of his wallet in his back pocket reminded him of

a conversation he'd had with Chance Reyes, a lawyer who had been involved in a high-profile case he'd worked on in December that had centered around Monty Powell as the prime suspect. The situation had taken a deadly twist and Waylon had ended up helping rescue Chance's sister, who had been kidnapped.

Waylon took out his wallet, removed the embossed business card on textured card stock, and stared at the printed words: Ironside Protection Services.

On the back, handwritten, was the direct personal line of the owner. The company had offices from the Rocky Mountains to the Great Plains. Chance had told the founder of the company, Rip Lockwood, about him, sang his praises, and extended an offer of employment if Waylon was ever interested. He had dismissed it. Recently, he'd been promoted to the rank of lieutenant. His reputation was unimpeachable. He had a home at the LPD.

Not being a law enforcement officer, starting over from the bottom, working his way up, proving himself to new people, hadn't been something he wanted.

Still wasn't.

But Melanie was right. Why did she have to be the one to sacrifice?

He needed to figure out what he wanted more. His home with the LPD. Or to be with Melanie. A woman determined to push him away. He didn't even know whether she loved him, and if she did, would it be enough? Would she ever put him first in her life, ahead of her ambition? Would she ever find balance between her job and having a family?

Did she even want to when she thought they were *doomed to fail*?

The bathroom door opened. Steam wafted out, followed by Melanie. "Ready to go?" Her tone strictly business.

He slipped the card in his wallet, shoved it in his pocket and opened the door for her as his answer.

As they walked to the outdoor staircase, she pointed to a beat-up old pickup truck parked between the ice machine and the stairs. "That's Kristin's truck. Wonder how long she's been back. I hope she wasn't afraid to call, thinking we fell asleep."

He put his hand on the hood. "It's cool. She's been back for a while. Maybe she was tired and decided to wait until the morning."

"Only one way to find out."

They made their way to the second floor and headed down the walkway.

The door to Room 204 was ajar. He put his hand out, stopping Melanie and putting her behind him. "Wait here." Drawing his weapon, he nudged the door wide open with his boot. "Kristin Loeb? It's Detective Wright and ADA Merritt. Are you in here?"

He stepped inside. The curtains were drawn. Moonlight cascading in from the open door provided the only light. Scanning the room, he took in the signs of a struggle. Broken lamp. Bedspread askew. One sandal on the carpet beside a cell phone. He crept around to the other side of the bed.

His gaze fell to a circle of sand. Two feet in diameter with an impression of an angel in the center. He ran to check the bathroom, only to confirm what he already knew.

Cursing, he hung his head as anger stabbed his chest. He stepped out of the bathroom and glanced at Melanie. "I think he's taken her. Call 9-1-1."

Chapter Ten

The Mile-High City Motel buzzed with activity, swarming with the police.

Melanie stood beside Waylon, along with Detective Stoltz from the Denver PD, who she wasn't familiar with, and watched the replay of the surveillance footage outside the motel.

Kristin pulled into the lot at ten forty. A white cargo van followed close behind. The driver parked two spots down from her truck and watched her walk to her room, then repositioned in front of the staircase. The license plate had been removed, but at least they could tell that it wasn't the same type of vehicle as the passenger van used by the FCTC.

A man dressed in black, wearing a motorcycle helmet, climbed out. He had on a backpack, probably containing the sand and doll he'd used to make the angel impression. Taking the steps two at a time, he hurried up to the second floor. He put his gloved left hand up to the peephole, blocking the view, and knocked with his right hand.

Kristin opened the door, almost without delay. He hit her, knocking her backward, deeper into the room, and stalked inside, shutting the door behind him.

"Wonder why she just let him in like that?" the detective said. "Without verifying who it was, especially since it was so late."

"She probably thought it was us knocking on the door." Melanie wrapped her arms around herself. Guilt gnawed at her. She and Waylon had been making love and arguing, distracted, when they should've been focused, on the lookout for Kristin. "We were supposed to meet up to discuss a lead she was following. Share information."

Now the killer had her. Because Melanie had indulged herself with Waylon.

On the playback, minutes later, the man carried Kristin out of the room, along with her messenger bag.

"All her notes, her digital voice recorder, her laptop was in that bag," Melanie said. "Kristin carried that stuff with her everywhere." Inside the room, they hadn't found any of her tapes or notebooks. Kristin only used a particular kind, leather hardcover in sky-blue, with an elastic band. She always had them on her.

"The last people to see Kristin Loeb were the Sand Angelites," Waylon said. "Either one of them followed her to the motel or they told whoever did where to find her."

"I'm not so sure." Melanie looked between the two detectives. "Kristin went to the press conference. The killer could have been there. He could've been following her since she left Pagosa Springs for all we know, if it's not Drake Colter."

The Denver detective stared at her with pity in his eyes, making her self-conscious of her black eye and the other disturbing marks on her face and neck. She wished she had purchased makeup from the drugstore to cover her bruises, but she hadn't been thinking of it at the time.

"We need to speak with the Angelites," Waylon said. "Do you know where to find them?"

"I have an address that was good three years ago." Melanie gave it to them. "Isaac Meacham owns the house. He inherited it from his father, along with a lot of money."

"Let's go talk to them. Find out what they discussed with Kristin," Waylon said. "On the way, can you give your Denver PD friend a call and see if Colter is at the FCTC?"

Javier Jimenez was a dedicated cop, currently watching the house.

"Hold your horses." Detective Stoltz raised a palm. "This is outside your jurisdiction, Wright, but you're welcome to accompany me to question the Angelites."

"I'm not going with you," Melanie said, and Waylon narrowed his eyes, probably sensing she was up to something. He knew her better than she liked at times. "I don't want to be anywhere near the Meacham house or the Angelites." Those people, with their gypsum necklaces, blue candles and spooky stares terrorized her, had driven her out of Denver. Their actions hadn't been violent, but they had been insidious and sinister. "I'll call JJ so he can make sure Colter's at the center, but then I'll head over to the FCTC so the two of us can question Kurt Parrish while I'm there."

She also needed to speak with Drake Colter. Alone.

That wasn't something Waylon was going to allow. As much as she tried to educate him about how he couldn't stop her from doing anything, the truth was, when he set his mind to a goal, including restricting her actions, nothing could deter him.

He had an iron will as formidable as hers.

Colter knew a lot more and had gone so far as to taunt them with the fact. If Waylon wasn't with her, that madman would think he had the upper hand and might let something vital slip.

She had to do this. For Kristin's sake.

"I don't like it." Waylon's voice was firm, his gaze drilling into hers. "Better if we stick together."

"Kristin is running out of time. Based on the last three victims, he'll keep her alive for twelve, maybe fourteen, hours before he kills her. It'll be faster if we split up. You know I'm right."

Waylon took her arm by the elbow and steered her across the room to a corner. "He's got Kristin," he said in a harsh whisper. "I can't let him get you, too." The affection in his voice tore at her heart.

After they'd found Kristin's empty motel room where the sand angel had been left on the floor as a message, Waylon hadn't hesitated to hold her, console her, as they'd waited for the police. Now, he was determined as ever to still protect her.

People often said a lot of things in the heat of an argument like the one they'd had earlier. But what a person did after was what really mattered. And when they did something meant to help someone else, without thinking about how it could benefit them, it resonated.

Waylon's actions, despite how she'd pushed him away touched her.

He was different than other men she had been involved with. What they shared was different, too. A far contrast from any of the carefully structured failed relationships she'd experienced.

"Kristin is alive," she said. "We have to do everything we can to save her. There are ten officers outside. I'm sure two of them can give me a ride to the FCTC. I'll stay with my friend until you pick me up or they take me to you. I won't be alone. I'll be fine."

His gaze hardened. "I still don't like it. A couple of beat cops playing chauffeur is one thing, but protecting you is something else, and I don't know this JJ."

"He's a competent, seasoned detective in a dangerous city with one of the highest homicide rates," she pointed out, willing to go so far as to list his commendations.

"That may be, but how do I know he isn't going to roll over for you, following any order you give him, no matter how reckless?" Waylon asked, raising an eyebrow like he sensed her plan. "Where you go, I go, remember."

Another tug on her heart. "We need to find Kristin before it's too late. If we don't, I'll never forgive myself." She put her hands on his chest. An affectionate gesture she never would've dared to risk doing in front of an officer back at home, but in

Colorado the same scrutiny didn't apply. She needed Waylon not to fight her on this. "The clock is ticking. We don't have time to waste. It'll be faster if we separate. Divide and conquer," she said, pleading with her eyes. "This isn't about JJ. This is about you trusting me."

He considered her for a moment and finally nodded, albeit reluctantly. "We check in with each other. Every twenty minutes. Text, phone call, something."

"Okay."

His brow still creased with worry. "Do you have one of your AirTags in this purse?"

"No." She'd opted for a Kate Spade leather bag, simple with a strap long enough for her to wear cross-body. It only cost two hundred dollars. Not thousands like some of her others. "But I've got my key chain that has one."

"Mind if I link it to my phone?"

She was willing to do whatever he wanted to put his mind at ease. "Not at all." She took it out of her purse to make pairing easier. After opening the Find My app on her own phone, she tapped the items tab, selected the AirTag located on her key chain and, under the share section, clicked on Add Person.

The rest was relatively straightforward and the process only took a couple of minutes. Now, he'd be able to track her in the event of a worst-case scenario.

Waylon turned to the other detective. "I need two officers to give her a ride to the Fair Chance Treatment Center. They need to stay with her until I get there, or they bring her to me."

Detective Stoltz nodded. "For the former ADA, I can make that happen. You put away a lot of bad guys, ma'am. At great personal risk, I might add. I remember hearing about what those Sand Angelites did to you. Horrible the way they harassed you. The least the Denver PD can do is keep you safe while you're back."

"Thank you," she said. It was nice to have her efforts recognized.

"Also, the perpetrator likes to leave his victims in sand dunes," Waylon said. "We need to have local authorities patrolling all of them throughout the state for the next twenty-four hours."

"That's a good idea." If the murderer couldn't access the dunes, it might buy Kristin more time.

Waylon bent down, pulled a revolver from the ankle holster hidden in his boot. "Take my BUG," he said, using the acronym for his backup gun, and handed it to her.

Melanie tucked the Smith & Wesson in her purse. She'd never been comfortable with guns until Waylon had insisted that she knew how to handle one properly and learn to shoot in case of an emergency.

With everything going on, being attacked at her job, the sand left on her doorstep and now Kristin kidnapped, this counted as an emergency. She was glad for the knowledge and the gun.

"Every twenty minutes," he said, reminding her.

"I'll be sure to check in. You do the same."

When Waylon had gotten overly protective of her in front of Colter, he had not only exposed himself but also the fact they were in a relationship or, at the bare minimum, that he had feelings for her. No telling who that killer had contacted and what details he had shared.

For all they knew, Colter considered Waylon a threat.

If he did, it would now make them both targets.

TWENTY MINUTES LATER, she was at the Fair Chance Treatment Center. She'd already fired off a text to Waylon and was speaking with Detective Javier Jimenez when she got a response.

Waylon: We're pulling up to the Sand Angelites house now. It's dark. They're either asleep, want to give that impression or aren't in there.

Waylon had taken his truck and followed behind Detective Stoltz. They'd wanted to get on the road and head back home once finished since they wouldn't be able to speak with Kristin.

Another chime.

Waylon: Be safe. Stay with the detective.

Melanie considered a reply but couldn't come up with an honest one that wouldn't raise his suspicion. Waylon had sharp instincts and a keen insight into her. Lying to him wasn't feasible. She'd only take the chance if she was willing to deal with his ire.

She chose no response as the best one and put her phone in her purse, leaving the handbag unzipped to give her easy access to the gun inside.

"No one has left the house since eight," Detective Javier Jimenez said as they spoke in front of FCTC. "At least, not from where I could see. Using the back alley is a possibility. As soon as I got your text about Kristin Loeb disappearing from her motel room, I checked. Drake Colter was in there. The motel is less than fifteen minutes away from here, with no traffic. It's possible he stashed her somewhere and made it back inside before I could verify that he was in the house."

They hadn't discovered Kristin was missing until eleven twenty. More than enough time for Colter to be the culprit.

"Of course, Drake Colter denies having any knowledge of what happened to Loeb," he said.

"Of course." Melanie shook her head, disgusted with the fact that a convicted murderer was on the loose and very well taking more innocent lives. "JJ, I hope they're paying you overtime for this."

"I wish." A half smile highlighted the wrinkles in his tan face. "My bigger concern is my wife. She's not happy with the extra hours on this now that we have two little ones."

Melanie patted his shoulder. She had no idea how he managed to juggle it all. Marriage, kids and this job. This work sucked away a small piece of one's soul. Took up most of their time and exposed them to the depths of darkness many civilians couldn't fathom.

Her thoughts careened back to Waylon. He understood her, accepted her in a way few ever had, including her parents. Unlike a lot of men she'd dealt with, he wasn't threatened by her confidence or blunt style. What they had was rare, but how could they ever make it work? Something would have to give for them to be together. Or more like *someone*. The prospect of her being the one to do the giving made her heart hurt. But the last several months without Waylon had been awful.

"What's the key to success? Is your wife a stay-at-home mom?"

"Nope. She's an ER nurse. The key is flexibility. Recognizing that we're not superheroes and getting lots of help. Her mom fills in when she can. Our siblings pitch in, too. The kids are with her sister tonight since my wife has a shift. It takes a village, right?"

"I suppose it does."

Melanie was an only child. Her parents were wealthy enough to bounce between the United States, Great Britain and India. Even if they lived closer, they weren't the pitch-in sort. She'd practically grown up in a boarding school, getting the best education their money could buy.

Waylon's family sounded warm and tight-knit, but no longer lived nearby.

Not that any of it mattered. She was the ADA and he was a top detective with the LPD. No point going down this rabbit hole. Some things weren't meant to be.

"Any updates in getting more eyes on the FCTC and Drake Colter," she said, refocusing the conversation to the business at hand.

"Since Kristin Loeb is now missing, the request to have

more bodies on the FCTC will be fast-tracked. We should have four officers posted around the clock within forty-eight hours."

That was a spot of good news. If only it took less time. "I'm going to go in. Talk to Parrish and Colter."

"I'll go with you. I told them to expect more questions tonight."

Having a detective at her side hadn't worked out earlier. She needed to do things differently. "I'd prefer it if you hung back out here."

JJ frowned. "Drake Colter is only out of prison because of a technicality. The man is dangerous."

"He is." Two simple irrefutable facts. "But he also likes his freedom. He's not going to lay a finger on me inside with you waiting for me out here." If for some reason she was wrong, then she had the revolver in her purse. "I think I can get more information out of him this way."

"Sure?" His skeptical tone indicated he was unconvinced her strategy was worth the risk.

"I'm sure." Even though she was aware Waylon would hate the idea. But he wasn't there to stop her.

"Have it your way, but I'll be right by the door, where I can hear every single word in case you need backup."

"All right." She went up to the front door with JJ. "When you questioned Parrish tonight, did you do it inside the house?"

"Yeah, why?"

"If he's helping Colter sneak out, I doubt he'd be likely to confess where Colter could be eavesdropping. I'll talk to him again down on the sidewalk. You hang by the door then. Okay?"

"Sure." JJ shrugged. "Let's try it."

Waylon was right. She pushed for what she wanted and everyone fell into line. The only one to ever push back and stand his ground was him.

Smiling at the realization, she rang the bell.

The door opened and she came face-to-face with a man.

Casually dressed in an open button-down plaid shirt over a cotton tee. Neatly trimmed dark hair and a mustache.

"Kurt Parrish, this is former Denver ADA Melanie Merritt," JJ said.

The man looked to be in his early forties, stood about five-ten or close to it, and was on the heavier side. His gaze roamed over her face. "What happened to you? Are you okay?"

"I was attacked. Possibly by Drake Colter, but most certainly by someone he knows."

Parrish's mouth twisted, his brow furrowing. "How can I help you?"

"I'd like to ask you a few questions. Would you mind stepping outside?" Without waiting for him to answer, she turned around and headed down the stairs.

The door creaked behind her and footsteps followed.

She waited for Parrish to join her on the sidewalk.

"I already told the detective over there that Drake Colter has been here all night," he said quickly.

"Yeah, I know. For all your shifts, Colter has been here. Present and accounted for."

"Exactly. That's right. I don't know what else I could tell you." He folded his arms across his chest and rubbed his chin.

"The truth. For starters." She eyed him, and Parrish opened his mouth to protest, but she continued. "Colter isn't finished with his hit list. The woman who was kidnapped tonight is on it. Along with myself. It's a matter of time before there'll be plenty of eyes on this house. Now is the time to come clean. To tell us the truth while we can still help you find a way out of this. Because detectives are going to start investigating you next."

"Me?" Parrish rocked back on his heels, his eyes growing wide as saucers. "But why? I haven't done anything wrong."

"Maybe. Right now, you're not the one in trouble. But I'm not sure it's going to stay that way."

Parrish raked a hand through his dark hair and flicked an uneasy glance back at the house.

JJ stood on the porch, keeping an eye on her as well as the foyer inside the FCTC.

"If Drake Colter has been leaving this house at night," she said, "and you've been covering it up for him, we're going to find out. It won't take much to get a search warrant and have a techie examine the digital record of your security system."

"We've had some problems with the system." He licked his lips and rubbed his chin again. "It's an old system that needs to be replaced. Everything that's happened with it lately is typical stuff. No one's fault. You can ask Hershel. He'll tell you the same thing."

Rambling, saying too much, was a key sign someone was lying. Either Kurt Parrish had tampered with the security system or he'd let Drake Colter meddle with it to hide his comings and goings.

"So I've heard. I bet those problems occurred on the same nights that women disappeared and were murdered. I'll go so far as to predict that it even happened tonight. If I'm right, it won't look good for you," she said, and his gaze dropped, bouncing around, like a man with something to hide, one trying to figure out what to do and say next. "This is a matter of life and death, Mr. Parrish. Time is running out for Kristin Loeb, who was taken tonight, and for you if you're helping Colter. Once we have evidence that you're lying, that you're aiding and abetting a serial killer, then you become an accomplice to murder. Then the DA's office will bring you up on charges, throw the book at you, and ensure you're doing time behind bars along with your close buddy, Drake Colter. You won't be shown any leniency."

Biting his bottom lip, Parrish blanched and looked almost sick. Glancing up at her, he folded his button-down shirt around himself. In the next breath, he smoothed it out again.

The movements were born of nerves, a way of stalling, giving himself time to think.

Melanie didn't rush him. She stayed still and quiet, studying him.

This was the moment where impatient cops and ADAs messed up by talking. Better to let him fill in the uneasy silence. Hopefully, with a confession.

"You're right, this is a matter of life and death, but I've got nothing else to say." Parrish's voice was shaky, his gaze refusing to focus. "I wish I could help you but…" Grimacing, he shook his head. "I can't. I'm sorry."

Parrish wasn't simply nervous. He was scared.

"We can protect you from him." She gestured toward the house with her head. "Keep you safe if you're worried telling us the truth will endanger you."

Parrish hesitated. Then he closed his eyes, squeezed his hands together and shook his head.

"Just talk to me," she said. "I can help get you immunity, but you've got to give me something to work with. Now, before Kristin Loeb is murdered."

"You can't help me." Opening his eyes, Parrish looked at her. Fear etched across his pale face. "I didn't do anything wrong. Drake Colter was here tonight and every night I've been on shift. Please leave me alone." He spun around and hurried up the steps, disappearing into the house.

Melanie released the breath she'd been holding along with her hope that Kurt Parrish would've caved so easily. She swore under her breath, berating herself for not pushing him harder. Kurt Parrish had cracked a little, letting his vulnerability show, but she'd needed him to break.

Looking at the Fair Chance Treatment Center, she couldn't afford to make the same mistake with Drake Colter.

Chapter Eleven

A Sand Angelite had finally opened the door, letting them into a surprisingly spacious entryway in the two-story Tudor-style house. The woman was young. Appeared to be no older than twenty-six, maybe twenty-seven. Probably still got carded in a bar. Blonde. Green eyes. Tall. Pretty. A shapely figure on display in a formfitting tank top, sans bra, and a tiny pair of shorts that left little to the imagination. She would've been his type before meeting Melanie.

Her name was Luna Tuttle. The woman showed them into the living room. She turned on a lamp and lit several blue candles, bending over seductively to do so, hoisting her bottom up in the air to draw their attention. Stoltz was captivated by her while Waylon chose to take in the modest décor of the room instead. She lit incense, a mix of patchouli and something cloyingly sweet. Then she left them and went to wake the others.

Stoltz and Waylon waited, his thoughts revolving around Mel. He reassured himself that she was with three officers, one of whom was a detective that she considered to be a friend. A pro and a con on that point. Whether or not JJ would roll over to her demands wasn't the issue. Trust was, and he needed to have some in her.

Melanie was competent, capable and armed.

She'll be fine.

Still, he was anxious to get through this and get back to

her. Seeing her, touching her, being in her presence, was the only thing that would truly ease his nerves.

Finally, all the Angelites had gathered in the living room and they could speak with them.

"This is Isaac Meacham," Luna said, introducing the last one to enter.

The deranged man who had broken into Mel's home and stripped away her peace of mind. He was around Drake Colter's age, mid to late thirties. With long curly hair and wearing a sky-blue tunic that matched the stone the entire group had either dangling around their necks or affixed to a bracelet, flowy linen pants and barefoot, he looked like his picture should be in a dictionary beside the definition of a cult leader.

Bringing his hands into a Namaste position in front of his chest, Isaac said, "What can we do for you at this late hour, Officers?"

"Detectives," Stoltz said, clarifying. He took out something to jot down notes. "Is this everyone?" Using his pen, he pointed around the room at the seven individuals huddled together. "Your entire group?"

"Our entire family is not present this evening," Isaac said. His voice gentle, his tone almost welcoming.

"How many of you are there?" Waylon asked, eyeing him.

Isaac smiled. "We are legion for we are many."

"Oh, brother," Stoltz said, taking the words from Waylon's lips. "So, would you say that's what…about ten? Twenty?"

Isaac shrugged. "It's hard to quantify legion."

Rolling his eyes, Waylon sighed. "Mr. Meacham, was Kristin Loeb here this evening?"

"She was."

Stoltz clicked the top button on his retractable ballpoint pen. "What did you discuss?"

"She asked questions and I answered them."

"What questions specifically?" Waylon pressed.

"There were so many, I don't recall." Isaac appeared bored or utterly serene, not a care in the world. "Perhaps you should ask Ms. Loeb."

"Unfortunately, we can't," Waylon said. "She was kidnapped earlier." He let that dangle, taking in their reactions. Bland. Unsurprised. Not a single one of them so much as batted a lash at the news. "You wouldn't happen to know anything about that, would you?"

"Why would I?" Isaac said, answering the question with another. "Or any of us, for that matter."

Stoltz cleared his throat. "Did you or any of your Angelites," the detective said, waving his pen around at the group, "have anything to do with her kidnapping?"

"We did not. My family, here before you, are peaceful. We do not inflict harm on others. We pride ourselves on being pacifists."

The specificity of the way he spoke struck Waylon as odd.

"Any idea why someone would want to kidnap her?" Stoltz asked.

Isaac clasped the blue stone sitting on his sternum between his thumb and index finger. "Ms. Loeb was an investigative journalist sticking her nose in all sorts of troubling things. Perhaps she was onto a story that angered the wrong person. Perhaps she was a sinner in need of redemption. Perhaps it was fate. I do not know. I suppose the only person who can say with any real certainty is the one who took her."

Shaking his head, Stoltz gave Waylon a look that screamed, *Can you believe this BS?*

The other Angelites either stood with their hands clasped or sat cross-legged on the carpet, all with unaffected expressions.

Stoltz jotted down the response from Isaac that didn't answer any of their questions. "What time did Kristin Loeb leave your house?"

"I'm not certain." Isaac eyed the little spiral notepad with a wary look. "We invited her to break bread with us. She left sometime after she was finished eating dinner." Isaac glanced around at the others. "Does anyone remember?"

"Eight thirty," Luna said quickly and Stoltz made a note.

Waylon studied her. "How can you be sure of the time?"

"She wanted to be somewhere before nine. I remember thinking she only had thirty minutes and needed to hurry."

If that was true, then the Sand Angelites might not have been the last ones to see and speak with Loeb. "She was pursuing something regarding a Savior. Or a Savior connection. Does that mean anything to any of you?"

The gaze of every Angelite swung to Isaac and they waited. It was the first time they'd done that. After the other questions, their attention had stayed focused on either Waylon or Stoltz.

This Savior thing meant something.

Isaac shook his head. "We have no idea what was going through her head. I wish we could be of more assistance."

Waylon seriously doubted that. "Have you or anyone in your *family* been in contact with Drake Colter?"

"Drake is with us at all times. In here," Isaac said, touching his forehead, "and here." He put a hand over his heart.

Waylon restrained a sigh. Frustration nipped at his nerves. "Did you visit him in prison?"

"The only true prison is that of the human body. A cage that falls to the wayside, turning to dust when we transcend from this world into the next."

Stoltz scratched his head. "What about since his release?" he asked, sounding equally as exasperated as Waylon felt. "Have you seen him in person, spoken to him on the phone?"

"His release was cause for celebration." Isaac held his hands out, palms up, a soft smile on his face. "We've all seen him to rejoice."

"When?" A hint of excitement made Stoltz's voice rise in

pitch as he turned the page in his notebook. "And where?" The detective waited with his pen poised above the paper.

"In the sacred space where the sands of time flow," Isaac said. "There we can see him, speak to him, connect with his spirit whenever we choose."

The other detective's shoulders sagged and he muttered something under his breath.

This was going nowhere. "Let's try this another way." Waylon tamped down his frustration and turned to Stoltz. "I'll take one outside. You grab another to question in the kitchen. Yeah?"

"Yeah. Otherwise this will take all night." Stoltz pointed to a frail-looking young man. "You, kid, what's your name?"

"Jovian."

"Show me to the kitchen. The rest of you stay here." The two headed off.

Before Waylon had a chance to single someone out, Luna Tuttle tapped his forearm, drawing his attention. "I wish to be of service. This way." She gestured for him to follow her and led him from the room, down the main hall in the opposite direction of the front door.

"Where are we going?"

Wide-eyed, she lifted a finger to her mouth and cast a wary glance back at the living room. Once they were further down the hall, she whispered, "There's something I need to show you. Away from the others." Her serene expression was gone. The young woman now looked spooked.

With groups like the Angelites, separating them and speaking confidentially tended to produce better results. Sometimes there was a weak link in the chain that could be broken; someone disgruntled, afraid, willing to talk once free of the scrutiny of the group.

Luna turned down a side hall, leading him to the first door

on the left. "It's in here. In my room." Opening a door, not too far from the entryway, she waved him inside with urgency.

The bedroom was bathed in candlelight. More cloying incense smacked him in the face, making him gag.

"This is an old house," she said. "The walls are thick. No one will overhear us in here." She hurriedly closed the door behind him.

"What did you need to show me?"

She padded over to a dresser near the door, opened the top drawer and took something out.

A small, sky-blue notebook. Leather-bound. Elastic band around it.

"It's Miss Loeb's."

Waylon took the notebook and thumbed through it. Lots of notes about the legal technicality that had resulted in Colter's release. Details from the press conference DA Jerk had given. Kristin had either watched it or had been there in person, which would've made sense since she'd driven up from Pagosa Springs. Notes on Isaac Meacham. The Angelites. The last thing written in the notebook was Meacham circled twice with an arrow drawn to Drake Colter. After that, several pages had been ripped out.

"Where did you get this?" he asked.

"Isaac gave it to me for safekeeping."

"Why give it to you?"

She shrugged, blank-eyed, a docile look on her face. "He often asks us to do things that require trust with no explanation."

"Did you tear out any pages from the notebook?"

"No. That's how I received it."

Slipping the notebook in his pocket, he moved to the other side of the room near the window, taking in her room. "Do you have any idea what this Savior connection that Ms. Loeb was interested in could be?"

"Drake Colter is a savior of sorts. Freeing sinners from this wicked world." She sashayed toward him slowly. "And Isaac is a different kind of savior. He found me living on the streets, addicted to drugs. He cleaned me up and gave me a home. A family. Saved me from the darkness inside myself. From the darkness in the world," Luna said, reinforcing the reasons for her to be loyal to the Angelites, making him wonder why she would betray Meacham's trust. "Maybe that's what she meant."

Doubtful. Whatever the connection, it wouldn't be straightforward and irrelevant. Loeb had stumbled onto something important. "Did Meacham ever visit Colter in prison?"

She eased closer, her beguiling manner, the candlelight and the bed making him uneasy. "I don't know. Isaac doesn't report to us."

"Did he ever give any of you orders that he said were directly from Drake Colter, on his behalf, or to help him in any way?"

"Isaac does not command us." Closing the distance between them, Luna invaded his personal space and he staggered backward into a corner. "He shepherds. Guides us to our purpose. Humbly asks for our service." Two more steps and she brought her body flush against his, her breasts brushing his chest.

"Whoa." He raised his hands, avoiding any inadvertent physical contact on his part, and scooted around her, putting several feet between them. "No touching, miss."

"What's wrong, Detective?" A guileful smile played on her lips. "I saw the way you looked at me after I let you in." Her innocent demeanor evaporated like smoke clearing. The woman was a chameleon, going from acolyte, to scared cultist, and now flirty minx. "Your spirit called mine. I was listening and I heard."

"There was no calling of anything to anyone." He'd been taken off guard by her skimpy attire, but he hadn't ogled, had kept his gaze above her neck and his focus solely on the job. "This is a misunderstanding."

"I don't think so. You're a man and I'm a woman. I can tell you're attracted to me. Your body is calling to mine. I'm an open vessel, willing to receive you. Rather than chase your tail in the darkness, why don't we commune without words instead." She pulled her tank top over her head and tossed it to the bed.

Waylon's pulse spiked as he averted his gaze. "We're done here. Go back to the living room." Spinning on his heel, he opened the door and hustled down the hall, looking for the other detective. "Stoltz!"

"In here."

Waylon followed his voice and the bright light to the kitchen, where he found the detective and the frail guy, thankfully, still clothed.

"You are the instrument of true violence," Jovian said, rubbing the stone attached to the bracelet on his right wrist. "Only when a sinner is released from the prison of their vessel can they begin to atone on a higher plane and find redemption. I cannot help you because you are lost in darkness. Destined to run in circles, blindly chasing your tail. Go in peace." Putting his hands in Namaste, he gave a slight bow and left the kitchen.

Stoltz turned to Waylon with a perplexed look. "Did you do any better?"

"The girl took off her top and asked to commune with me. Without words."

The detective's eyebrows shot up. "Why doesn't that kind of thing ever happen to me?"

"Consider yourself lucky." The detective would have to include that in a report whereas Waylon didn't have to worry about paperwork since this was technically on his personal time. He scrubbed a hand over his face, the ick factor about the incident with Luna Tuttle still bothering him, making him feel dirty, even though he hadn't done anything inappropriate. "I did get this from her," he said, handing over the notebook, "but I want to take pictures of the pages that are left."

"Left?"

"Several were ripped out." His guess was those pages contained the link they were looking for. "These Colter cultists aren't going to cooperate."

He took out his phone to check in with Melanie. They'd exceeded the twenty-minute mark. Easy for them both to get caught up and sidetracked while investigating. He refused to worry prematurely. It'd only anger her. He'd send a text and wait no longer than two minutes for a response. Then he'd worry.

"You're probably right," Stoltz said, "but we've got to question the rest of them."

True, but precious time would be wasted. They had to go about this in a different way.

Starting with getting a list of Drake Colter's visitors at the prison in Florence and copies of all the mail he received.

Chapter Twelve

Melanie finished collecting her thoughts and composed herself before heading to meet JJ at the front door. Another text came in.

Waylon: Only getting cultish drivel from these crackpots. Hope you're having better luck.

Taking a breath, she messaged him back. Let you know in a few minutes.

"Colter is waiting for you in the foyer," JJ said. "I'll be right here, and we're keeping the door open."

A tingle along the back of her neck urged her to use caution. She slipped the strap of her purse over her head, wearing it cross-body, and ensured the handle of the gun was within easy reach. She needed to push Colter as hard as possible. Regardless of the personal risk. It might be the only way to save Kristin.

Steeling herself, she stepped inside, closing the door enough to obscure JJ from Colter's sight, but cracked open so that the detective could overhear the conversation.

"ADA Melanie Merritt, you're back sooner than I expected." He stood leaning against the back wall, dressed in dark slim-cut jeans, a black long-sleeved Henley, with his hands in his pockets. His eyes narrowed. "Your face looks like it's been through a meat grinder. Your neck, too. Does it hurt?"

She noticed he didn't ask what happened. "Looks worse than it feels, but pain is fleeting," she said, wishing again that she'd purchased makeup.

"Perhaps that of the body, but what about the soul? It must hurt you, deep down, to keep losing people you collaborated with. People I can only presume are being killed because you tried my case with such vehemence. Not that I would know the perpetrator's true motives."

"Just a guess on your part, huh?"

A smug look crossed his face. "I see you took my advice and didn't bring the big fella, Detective Waylon Wright. Not that it isn't possible to bring a big guy such as him to heel. By the way, where is he?"

"Busy following a lead."

"I bet he's busy all right. Maybe he's found a pretty young thing, a lot warmer than you, to keep him occupied," he said and she tensed—an unexpected reflex. "But how is he supposed to keep you safe if he isn't here?"

Colter had shaved and showered since the last time she'd seen him. His hair no longer looked greasy, but clean. He had deceptive surfer-boy good looks. In the simple attire that could've come off the rack of Banana Republic or any upscale clothing store, he looked like a nice guy. The friendly next-door neighbor.

But she knew better. A monster lurked behind that cleaned-up veneer.

"I can take care of myself," she said, her tone conversational, and put a steady hand on her purse.

"Bet plenty of dead women said the same thing before they underestimated the wrong person. I wonder how many."

The words rattled her, making her wonder, too, for a second. "Tell me, do you often sleep in jeans and long sleeves in the summer?" she asked, needing to regain control of the line of questioning.

"I'm flattered you want to know what I sleep in, ADA Merritt. Would you like to come back to my bedroom, take a private peek at my pajama drawer, and get to know one another better on a first-name basis?"

"I'll pass, but I'm sure Detective Jimenez would be interested in having a look."

A half grin tugged at his mouth. "I changed my clothes and put this on after Kurt woke me from a *deep sleep* to let me know the cops were here. I heard Kristin Loeb is missing. Wish I could say it's such a shame, but I didn't particularly care for her."

"Did you take her?"

"I don't understand how that would be possible." His devilish eyes gleamed with amusement. "I've been here all night."

"Then you know who did, don't you?"

That grin spread into a vile smile. "I'm under no obligation to answer your questions."

"Don't you want to cooperate?"

He pushed off the wall and stalked toward her. The stench of menthol cigarettes wafted from him, and a chill slithered down her spine. "Why would I? I've already admitted that I didn't care for her."

"Was that her sin? Upsetting you? Getting under your skin? Was that the sin of your first victims, too?"

"Weakness is a sin in my book. But a necessary one in the circle of life."

Only someone sick and evil could rationalize cold-blooded murder. "There isn't a drop of remorse in you, is there?" she asked, stricken by his twisted mind.

"Hard to feel bad about a rabbit being prey for a wolf. It's in a predator's nature to hunt, to kill the weak and vulnerable. Those bunnies with their bushy tails are so cute, so soft, their bones so fragile. They frighten easily, and I think it's that fear that a wolf enjoys most. Or maybe it's the hunt. How that craving builds and builds during the chase, expanding with every breath, the excess seeping from the pores, making his mouth water with anticipation of the kill."

Melanie's nerves tightened and she did everything in her power not to let it show. "Kristin isn't a rabbit, and she isn't weak."

"Wasn't she?"

Melanie's stomach clenched. *Wasn't.* He was talking about her in the past tense. Not a good sign. Was she already dead?

Colter pushed up his shirtsleeve and turned his arm so the list of names was upright for her to see. "Six people stole something from me. Three years of my life. A cardinal sin that demands the sweetest kind of retribution. Not that I would dream of seeking it."

She kept her expression sterile. "You're a serial killer. Kristin didn't steal anything from you any more than I did. It's called justice." Melanie raised her chin, not letting her gaze waver from him for a second despite the fear prickling her. "She's a brave woman. Had the courage to show the world who you really are."

"You think you know me. You don't." Eyes narrowing, he shook his head in a slow eerie manner and tipped his head to the side, reminding her of the man wearing the helmet who had attacked her. "Not yet. But you will. Soon." He took a step closer, keeping his hands in his pockets. "Very soon and then you'll learn you're not in control of this situation. No matter how much you mistakenly think you are."

Her chest constricted with fear and anger, but she couldn't let him dare think he was getting to her. "I know exactly who you are. What you are. A murderer. A liar. A coward." Melanie watched him, noting the slight twitch of his mouth, the hard set of his jaw. She was getting to him. *Good.* She just needed to push a bit harder. "And when this is over, you're going to be back where you belong. Rotting behind bars in a supermax prison for the rest of your life."

"For a dead woman walking, you've got a lot to say."

She fought back a shudder just as JJ stormed inside the house. He shoved the front door so hard it banged against the wall. She grimaced at him. He was too soon.

Two more minutes alone with this animal was what she needed.

"All right, Colter, that sounded like a threat to me," the detective said. "Maybe we should take a ride down to the station and continue this chat in an interrogation room."

Colter smirked. "I assure you that was not a threat, Detective Jimenez. Now a real threat would've been something more forceful," he said and shifted his gaze from the cop to her. "I don't know, maybe something like, 'I'm going to wrap my hands around your throat and choke the life out of you, and when it's over I'm going to fill that smart mouth of yours with sand and walk away scot-free.'"

A ball of dread dropped into her stomach.

JJ grabbed Colter and threw him up against the wall, smashing the side of his face against the plaster.

"Hang on, Detective, that was just for instance," Colter said, raising his hands in submission. "I was giving you an example of a threat to show you the difference. That's all. No harm done. I would never dare threaten her seriously. And certainly not with witnesses in earshot. I was well aware you were on the other side of that door the entire time, listening. Are you sure you want to do the paperwork of hauling me in? 'Cause my lawyer is going to bring a few news cameras with him when he shows up to have me released. He's got them on speed dial, and I gave him a heads-up after you knocked on the door earlier."

JJ looked over his shoulder back at her. His silent question hung in the air.

Melanie wanted Drake Colter in jail and for a lot longer than three days. Patience was hard, but key. She shook her head.

With a frown, JJ let him go.

"I'm glad to see reason prevail." Colter brushed off his clothes. "I think I'm going to head back to bed." He stretched and yawned as if tired. "Next time, if you have any more questions for me, I'll consider answering them with my lawyer present. Or maybe I won't. Let you *keep chasing your bushy tail*. So much more fun. You have a good night, ADA Merritt. Sleep tight and watch out for those sand bugs because they bite." Colter sneered at her before turning around and stalking off down the hall.

Seething, Melanie tramped out the door and marched down the stairs.

JJ was right behind her. "Why didn't you want me to haul him in?"

She bristled at him questioning her decision as she headed over to his car. "I'd rather give him enough rope to hang himself." Colter was too cocky, too damn sure of himself and whatever plan he'd cooked up. It was only a matter of time before he made a huge mistake. She only hoped it would be sooner rather than later and that they'd be able to save Kristin. The podcaster had hours, not days. "You should've given me two more minutes with him."

"Rather than you provoke a murderer, I should take him in. We could hold him for up to seventy-two hours," he said, telling her what she already knew. "Plenty of time to see if Kristin Loeb's DNA is on his clothes."

"If he took Kristin, he didn't do it wearing that outfit." Surely he would've disposed of the clothes he'd worn while committing a crime. That was how they'd got him last time. His DNA on the victim and that of the victim's found in his apartment.

"How do you know?"

"Because he's smarter than that. Learned from his past mistakes." Colter could play the part of the fool when he wanted, come across as uncouth, the way he had earlier today, wearing the wife-beater, probably to fit in better with the other men in the house. She'd seen him do it before in front of a jury, acting meek and docile, as though he wouldn't hurt a fly. But that animal had an IQ of 120. Only fifteen points shy of hers. Underestimating him would be a mistake. "He expected us to come here tonight. Just like he expected a visit from the police after the other three women turned up dead. This is a game to him. Every single move he's made, including requesting to be placed in a halfway house to give himself an alibi, is a part of it." She drew a cleansing breath. "He's behind this and he's getting help. We need the police on the front and back of the house, day and night. Wherever he goes, we need eyes on him."

"That's already in the works. There has to be something else. Another angle to pursue. Another way to nail that scumbag. How do we beat him at his own game?"

This *was* a game to him, but other pieces were on the board. They needed to focus on those. The most vulnerable ones. "Kurt Parrish. He's scared. He's also lying and covering for Colter for some reason. We need to know what it is." Then a thought occurred to her. "Before a prisoner is released, how far in advance are they notified of what halfway house they're going to be placed in?"

"I'm not sure," JJ said with a shrug. "In regular circumstances, a year's notice, but with Colter's odd situation, much less. Maybe a month or two beforehand."

Released prisoners assigned to a halfway house could also request a specific area, to be closer to friends, family, a support system, which would narrow down the options to one or two places before he knew for certain.

"Long enough for him to have someone figure out the best

person to exploit over here at the FCTC. Look into Parrish's financials, question his family and friends to see if anything has changed in his life recently. Whatever leverage Colter is using, whatever hold he has on Parrish, we need to find it. Use pressure to make Parrish crack. He came close tonight." So close, she could taste it. She rubbed her temple, trying to figure it out. "I need you to speak to the other men that live in there. But away from the center, without Colter knowing. If Colter is sneaking out with Parrish's help, someone inside knows about it. We need to get them to talk."

"Too bad your investigator, Vasquez, isn't available."

He was the best at what he did. "Have you heard anything about Emilio?"

"Yeah, he's alive and well. On a cruise with his wife. According to the sister-in-law, they get back early tomorrow."

Knowing Emilio, and how driven he had been on the Sand Angel Killer case, he would be eager to investigate, putting himself in harm's way.

"After what happened to Kristin," she said, "he and his family will need police protection." Despite not letting Colter see how much this weighed on her, it did. She couldn't help but feel somewhat responsible for the three deaths and Kristin's disappearance. Vasquez and his loved ones could still be safeguarded.

"He's not the only one who needs protection," JJ pointed out, "You're not safe here, or in Wyoming, by the looks of your face. Maybe you should take some time off, lay low somewhere far away until we can get to the bottom of this."

"I ran once. I won't do it again." Instead of running scared, she should be used as bait, to lure Colter or the copycat killing innocent people for him. Not that Waylon would ever agree to such a plan. "I need to see this through. Besides, I have a job back home that I have to do."

"Some things never change." JJ exhaled a heavy breath. "Then you need protection, too. Around the clock."

"Kristin is the one we need to worry about right now. Not me." If anything happened to the investigative journalist because she'd let her guard down in a moment of weakness with Waylon, she'd never forgive herself. "I'm covered. I've got strict instructions to either stay with you or have those guys," she said, gesturing to the patrol officers who had given her a ride over to the FCTC, "take me to my bodyguard."

She understood the need to be protected, but all the forced proximity with Waylon made it impossible for her to compartmentalize her messy emotions where he was concerned.

Confronting how she felt about Waylon, taking on the pressure of his feelings for her, and coping with this nightmare of Drake Colter at the same time was pushing her limits of what she could handle.

Her personal drama had to be set aside.

Stopping Colter and finding Kristin needed to be her sole focus.

"Why isn't this bodyguard with you?" JJ asked. "Where is he now?"

"Questioning the Sand Angelites." Something she was happy not to do. They were a bunch of fanatics who made her skin crawl. Those weirdos were willing to go to great lengths for Drake Colter, including stalking her and breaking into her home.

Yet they had never harmed her physically.

Isaac Meacham could've tried to kill her that night in her house instead of sitting like a passive yogi, holding a blue candle. Aside from freaking her out and making a ghastly mess, he hadn't even done any real damage to her property. The sand and walls had been cleaned up and, after a fresh coat of paint, no one could tell what had happened. That night, Isaac hadn't uttered a single word. Not one threat. Hadn't resisted arrest.

But could she be wrong about the Angelites? Were they more than creepy cultists?

Were the Sand Angelites killers, puppets, working under Drake Colter's influence?

She had to puzzle it out, find the answers before Kristin Loeb ran out of time.

Chapter Thirteen

The clock on the dash read four ten. Two hours before dawn broke. It was still dark outside.

Waylon exited off Interstate 25 rather than take it farther north to I-80, which would have nighttime roadwork until six. He'd decided to take the shortcut instead that would save them close to an hour of driving and get them home that much sooner. It had been a long, draining night and they were both in dire need of rest.

He hit the ramp on to the smaller US Route 287 headed north. They hadn't gotten any sleep, but the good thing about the early hour, no traffic was on the road. The lane in front was clear and there was no one behind them.

Sweet darkness.

The lack of traffic and the roadwork on I-80 were the only reasons he'd chosen the shortcut that he didn't dare use during rush-hour congestion. US 287 was known for accidents at peak hours due to tired truckers, students going between Colorado State University and Southeastern Wyoming University, and a lack of passing lanes, but now they practically had it to themselves.

He preferred the route for expediency and, when the sun was up, for the breathtaking scenery.

They were still in Colorado but had already passed Fort Collins and were less than an hour from home, drawing closer to the Wyoming border every second.

With all the time they'd spent on the road in the past twenty-four hours, he wished they had been in Melanie's luxury cross-over with plush leather seats and fully functional A/C instead of his old GMC that had more than a hundred and seventy-five thousand miles on it. She would've been far more comfortable.

Not that she had complained.

Despite the fact she preferred the finer things in life, she was always at ease with the simple way he lived. Never a snide remark or backhanded compliment. He'd gotten that from other women on occasion. Mel might be sophisticated, and he'd wondered if they'd get along outside of bed in the early days because of it, but she wasn't snooty.

He'd never put up with a snob, or anyone who thought the rules didn't apply to them because of money, much less consider rearranging his world for someone like that.

Waylon glanced over at her. She was still awake. The tension that had been in her shoulders had faded away and her features were relaxed.

But they were both restless.

For him, it wasn't simply that he was driving or worried about her safety. He hadn't shared every detail of how things had gone with Stoltz at Isaac Meacham's house. Keeping secrets from someone he cared about wasn't his style. He was more of an open book, making him wonder why he hadn't spit it out already.

"I need to tell you something that happened at the house when we were interviewing the Sand Angelites. It's nothing really." Though it felt like a big icky something. "It might upset you, but it shouldn't." Honestly, he didn't have a clue whether it would bother her. Their status was still in limbo and a big question mark remained regarding how she felt about him.

Head resting against the seat, Mel turned, looking at him. "What is it?"

"One of the Angelites, a young woman named Luna Tuttle, kind of, sort of, cornered me."

"Cornered you?" she asked. "I don't understand. Was she a big woman who felt like she could take you on? That doesn't sound like them. I've never known them to be violent or physically aggressive."

He needed to be concise, matter-of-fact. "Cornered me in a bedroom."

One brow raised, head slightly inclined, Mel looked as aloof as royalty. "Go on."

"She took off her top, with nothing underneath. Basically, offered to have sex with me."

Melanie's gaze fell.

"It made me uncomfortable, and I got out of there."

She squirmed in her seat, fidgeting with her hands, and glanced out the passenger's-side window.

He waited for her to say something. Anything. When she didn't, he thought it best to move on, "There's one thing about the Sand Angelites that keeps bugging me."

"Don't you mean one *more* thing? Luna Tuttle making a pass at you in a bedroom that you never should've been in, I take it with the door closed, would be one thing." Her tone sounded more annoyed than accusatory. Then she said, "It figures. Only a matter of time."

"What is that supposed to mean?"

"Nothing."

That was very much something. "What's only a matter of time?"

"You disappointing me." She shook her head. "Not that I have any right to be upset that some pretty young thing scrambled your brain. Even though we just had sex a couple of hours beforehand."

Being this upset meant she cared deeply. "You heard the part where I didn't do anything and left the room?"

"I heard you." She folded her arms. "How many women have you slept with since we met?" She took a quick breath and waved a hand. "Never mind. I don't want to know. We were never officially exclusive anyway."

Weren't they? Isn't that the reason they'd stopped using condoms while she stayed on the pill. "I haven't been with anyone else since that night you came home with me from Crazy Eddie's. Not even while we were on a break." He thought about that, how important details and transparency were to her. "Well, I did have dinner with a couple of women after you stopped returning my calls, but that was the extent of it. I never even kissed them."

"You're free to do what you want," she said flippantly.

"What I want is you, Mel. Have you been with other guys?"

Silence descended for too many painful heartbeats.

"No," she finally said. "I've been too busy working and I know better than to get cornered in a bedroom."

She was right. He should've been smarter.

The moment the Tuttle woman led him to her room, a red flag should've flashed in front of him. But he'd honestly thought she was going to break ranks from the Angelites, betray them, and give him some information that might save Kristin Loeb. His guard had been down around her. She was demure. Clearly not a threat, at least not in the typical way. And, well, pretty. Silly that attractiveness could be weaponized, used against his defenses, but it had been.

"I can understand questioning the Angelites separately, isolating them from the group, which makes sense, but did you choose this Luna Tuttle to speak to, or did she volunteer?" Melanie asked, still not looking at him.

He replayed it in his head. "Tuttle volunteered."

"She targeted you, Detective. You were a sucker for an attractive woman and acted against your better judgment, which is what bothers me." She kept staring out the window at the dark landscape, trees lining the highway, and the approaching mountains. "Like I said, Tuttle is one thing. Now you've got something else. Are you sure there aren't more than two things? We are talking about the Angelites."

"Okay, there is a lot, but at the top of the list is something a couple of them said."

"Let me guess. Was it about sinners and redemption? Or maybe something to do with how we're lost in darkness and only they can see clearly?"

"They both made remarks about us *chasing our tails*. Odd, right, that they would both use the same turn of phrase, in separate rooms, at different times? Can't be a coincidence."

Stiffening, Melanie finally looked at him. "Since we're sharing things that might upset the other, it's my turn." Something in her tone made him brace himself. "Drake Colter used similar words about me chasing my tail when I spoke to him at FCTC. Alone."

Anger flared hot and Waylon clenched the steering wheel. "You did what?"

"Before you blow a gasket, hear me out. I don't think it's a coincidence that Colter and the Angelites used the same words. I think it was deliberate. To send us a message that he's the one in control. I also think he spoke to the Angelites. Told them to anticipate a visit from you. Had this Tuttle woman make a sexual overture toward you to mess with me."

The last part drew his gaze. "Why do you think that?"

"Because he flat-out said that you weren't with me because you were busy with a pretty young woman who was warmer and more open than me."

He'd been lured to the room as part of a ruse, set up to be seduced. But why?

Melanie huffed a breath. "It prickled me when he suggested the idea and stung to hear you confirm it. I don't know why I'm letting that evil monster push my buttons," she said and

Waylon wondered if it had been done simply to hurt Mel. "Colter must've spoken to Isaac Meacham or someone else at their house after we saw him this afternoon. Orchestrated the whole thing. That's the only explanation for…"

High-beam headlights popped on behind them. Waylon put a hand up to his eyes against the harsh glare of sudden bright light that had materialized out of nowhere. He would've sworn nobody had been behind them, and he'd been checking, but if the person had been driving without their headlights on after the turn onto US 287, he wouldn't have seen them.

"What the heck?" Melanie turned, looking out the back window.

Waylon's focus shot to the rearview mirror.

The vehicle accelerated fast, getting a lot closer, too close, in a span of a few seconds. The driver must've floored it.

This was a two-lane highway, with only one for each direction that didn't widen until after they had gotten beyond the mountains. There were lots of bends on the road. With the straightaway looming ahead, maybe the other driver wanted to pass them now, but it didn't appear he or she was moving into the other lane.

Waylon put on his hazard lights, hoping it would encourage them to go around. Instead, the other vehicle zoomed up, coming right at them, and rammed the back of his truck.

His GMC jolted violently, jostling them forward in their seats.

Melanie gasped. "They're trying to run us off the road!"

"Or kill us," he said tightly.

Either was bad news that didn't bode well for them. He pressed down on the gas, going past the speed limit of sixty-five. The engine strained at eighty. With no oncoming traffic, he dared to cut across the yellow line into the adjacent lane, and the other vehicle followed.

The van, possibly another truck—hard to tell with the blinding glare of the high beams—exceeded their speed, eating the distance between them, catching up quickly.

An edge caught in his throat. The vehicle plowed into them again, rocking his truck harder than the last time they'd been hit and forcing him to swerve.

Gripping the seat and bracing a hand on the dash, Mel glanced over at him. "Can you outrun them?"

His old GMC Sonoma was reliable, compact, useful for hauling large objects that weren't too heavy, like appliances and lumber. Small enough to maneuver through tight spaces, but his truck was tiny and light compared to heftier ones. The vehicle behind them was larger, heavier and more powerful than his.

No way he could outrun the other driver.

Waylon wrestled the wheel as they veered back over the yellow line into the correct lane and he managed to bring the truck back under control. "Not in this thing."

"How long do you think they've been following us?" she asked.

"I don't know." Waylon cursed and shook his head. "My guess is since I left Meacham's house."

"But the Angelites aren't violent."

He pressed down on the accelerator, trying to avoid another hit. The chassis rattled and the engine whined when he pushed it to ninety. Waylon glanced at the dashboard just as the oil pressure icon started blinking. The truck wouldn't take much more of that.

"They could've easily followed me after we finished talking to them at Meacham's house."

"And they could've also told someone else where you were when you questioned them separately. Or it could've been Colter. Maybe he called his friend who's helping him kill people. You picked me up right in front of the FCTC. I was outside for a while with JJ before you showed up."

The vehicle was closing the distance once more.

Waylon was ready or did his best to be. The big vehicle slammed into them. He jerked the wheel hard, using the weight of his GMC Sonoma to hold his ground. The other automobile backed off, falling behind a couple of yards.

But he knew it wouldn't last.

The pavement offered no shoulder and they neared a particularly treacherous curve in the winding road. He'd have to slow down to a safe speed. No other choice. On the west side of the highway was a towering mountain wall of solid rock. On the east was a sheer drop-off. He couldn't remember how far down and, in the dark, he couldn't tell. Why had he taken the chance with the shortcut?

This section of Route 287, cutting around the mountain, was perilous, dubbed the "highway of death." The driver had timed the attack on them perfectly. Waiting until they'd reached the most dangerous point.

Who the heck was behind the wheel?

Drake Colter was no doubt responsible, but he wasn't so foolhardy as to be driving with attention laser-focused on him after Kristin Loeb had been taken last night. Had he sent Isaac Meacham, another Sand Angelite, or someone else after them?

The driver switched off the high beams and Waylon swore. They wouldn't be able to see the next hit coming until it was too late.

An engine roared up behind them. The growling sound grew louder as it closed in.

Waylon slowed for the curve but cut the wheel hard, veering back over into the oncoming lane, toward the side of the mountain. He came within inches of skimming the driver's side against the rock.

He didn't know which would be worse, colliding into the jagged wall of rock, smashing into an oncoming vehicle, or crashing into old guardrails that might be weakened by corrosion or destabilized by the highway shoulder beneath it.

Grimly, he decided the guardrail with a looming cliff-side drop might be worse.

Melanie leaned toward him, her face tense, her eyes filled with fear. He had to get her out of this in one piece, unharmed.

The vehicle rammed into their rear bumper. It was all Waylon could do to keep from wiping out on the rock wall. Rather than crash into the side of the mountain, he cranked the wheel, taking them back over into his lane just as they came out of the deadly curve of the road, clearing the peak of the drop-off, and hit a straightaway.

Up ahead, the highway was dark and clear of other cars.

While Waylon focused on keeping his GMC on the road, the vehicle behind them pulled around and raced up along the back of the driver's side. In the side mirror, Waylon caught a glimpse of the outline. A behemoth truck that outmatched his in every way—size, weight, engine, horsepower.

The dark-colored truck crashed into them as Waylon whipped the wheel to the left, turning into the hit. The vehicles locked, clashing like steel beasts. He struggled to maintain control. Metal screeched against metal, the mechanical screams grating like fingernails on chalkboard.

Swearing under his breath but otherwise maintaining his composure, Waylon eased his foot down on the brake pedal, hoping to unlock them. He didn't dare jam it to the floor and risk sending the GMC into a deadly spin.

The tires grinded against asphalt, the smell of burning rubber filled the air. His truck shuddered. Finally, the other driver jerked them apart, but Waylon's GMC fishtailed.

He sped up, desperate to try and make it to the next exit before they were hit again.

Too late.

The other vehicle sideswiped them. This time sending his

truck into a skid. He tried to steer into it, but he couldn't recover. In spite of Waylon's best efforts, the skid became a sickening spin.

"Waylon!"

"Brace yourself," he said, turning the wheel in the direction the vehicle wanted to go, which was his only hope of regaining control.

As if the truck had a mind of its own, the GMC rotated three hundred and sixty degrees, careening toward the edge. Instinctively, he reached out, putting an arm across Melanie, doing anything he could to protect her while keeping his other hand on the steering wheel.

They smashed into the guardrail and steel shrieked.

Chapter Fourteen

Melanie's teeth clattered together hard enough to ignite sparks of pain in her jaw, shooting all the way into her temples. The seat belt, which stretched diagonally across her chest from right shoulder to left hip, instantly cinched so tight that her breath was wrenched from her.

Their truck rebounded from the guardrail, not with enough momentum to cause them to collide with the other vehicle but with so much torque that they spun in a full circle again.

Waylon jerked the steering wheel back and forth erratically, fighting for control. Melanie struggled to orient herself.

As they came out of the second three-hundred-and-sixty-degree rotation, the other vehicle struck them, plowing into the driver's side. She didn't see it coming, only felt the blow that knocked the breath from her lips and sent them crashing into the guardrail once more.

She turned toward Waylon. Past his window, she looked through the windshield of the other vehicle and saw the driver.

The man wearing a black helmet revved the engine of the full-sized truck. The front fender of the massive vehicle didn't lose contact with Waylon's door, directing all that horsepower, forcing their vehicle deeper into the guardrail. The larger truck shoved them five or maybe ten feet.

A grinding-scraping of metal on metal. A flurry of golden sparks bursting up like a swarm of summer fireflies against the dark sky.

Their truck began to pitch to the right. The guardrail was giving way.

No. No!

She glanced below, out her window, her heart in her throat. Through the darkness, she could make out a steep slope and trees, but had no way of knowing how far down the drop was or what was at the bottom.

Steel buckled, and with a rending screech the guardrail cracked apart. In a jangle of detached posts and railings, the truck slipped sideways along the embankment.

Melanie's stomach twisted with nausea. Even though she was restrained by the seat belt and Waylon had thrown his arm across her body instinctively, she pressed her right hand against the door and her left against the dashboard, bracing herself.

Gravel and dirt spewed into the air. Their truck continued in a bumpy, jarring slide down the slope. As it was happening, she couldn't believe it. Her brain registered the tumble toward death while her heart stubbornly clung to hope.

Then the embankment grew steeper and the truck flipped over.

A scream tore from Melanie's lips. Her belt jerked painfully against her chest. Their descent was fast and hard. Gasping for breath, pulse pounding like a drum in her ears, she wrenched painfully from side to side in the harness of the seat belt.

She prayed for a sturdy tree, a spur of rock, something to stop their fall.

The headlights sliced the darkness. She wasn't sure how many times the truck rolled—maybe only three times—because up and down had lost all meaning.

Her head banged into the cab ceiling so hard it nearly knocked her out. She couldn't tell if she'd been thrown upward or if the roof had dented inward. Trying to slump in her seat, terrified the ceiling might crumple further on the next roll, she worried for Waylon, who was so much bigger than she, that his skull might be crushed.

The windshield shattered, showering the safety glass. The headlights blinked off.

His truck rolled onto its roof again but slipped farther into the seemingly bottomless ravine with a thunderous, clattering roar. Her life flashed before her eyes, full of emptiness, regrets, fears, despite her fearless façade. All the things she'd never said and should have.

The GMC whooshed to the bottom, bounced, landing upright on its wheels, the back end crashing into something, bringing them to a merciful halt.

Thank you.

Her head spun. The sound of rushing water filled her ears.

The river. They'd stopped inches from it.

She turned to Waylon. The dashboard lights were still on, reflecting his sweat-slicked face and closed eyes.

"Waylon?" Her voice was hoarse.

He was slumped over in his seat, only held up by the seat belt, head bent toward her, resting against his shoulder.

She touched his face. "Waylon."

He didn't move. Something warm and sticky covered his right temple and cheek.

Blood.

Her heart squeezed. Dread thrummed in her veins.

Please, be alive. I don't want to lose you.

With trembling fingers, she touched him just under his nose. A sob of relief punched out of her when she felt the warm exhalation of his breath.

Waylon was unconscious. Not dead.

Fumbling with the release mechanism on her seat belt, she had to get him out of there. Head injuries were dangerous. He needed medical attention as soon as possible.

The safety harness disengaged and she freed herself from the entangling straps. She groped around for her purse. Found it and called for help.

Once finished explaining to the 9-1-1 operator, she put the phone on the dash.

"A highway patrol officer will be to your location momentarily, ma'am, and an ambulance has been dispatched. I'll remain on the line with you."

"Thank you," she said, her voice shaky. "But he's still not conscious. I don't know what to do." Her throat constricted.

"Help is on the way, ma'am. Stay calm."

Melanie pressed her hands to Waylon's cheeks, cradling his face. "Don't die," she whispered in his ear. "I love you. Please stay with me." Tears welled in her eyes. "Wake up. Please, wake up. I can't lose you." Panic fluttered in her chest. What if he never regained consciousness? What if she did lose him? He'd been out too long. How were emergency services going to reach them once they arrived? "Waylon! I order you to wake up. Right now."

As if on command, he roused with a grunt. His head lolled. Then he opened his eyes, his gaze taking in their surroundings before finding hers. "Are you all right?" he asked, reaching for her.

He was alive and awake. She was going to be fine.

Hot tears rolled down her cheeks. "Yes, I'm okay." She wrapped her arms around his neck and held him tight.

They'd come so close to dying. Too close.

No matter how hard she tried to ignore her feelings for him, to keep some semblance of emotional detachment, she just couldn't do it any longer.

She couldn't walk away from him again. Couldn't spend the rest of her life aching to be near him.

But could she give up the one thing in her life that gave her a sense of purpose for him?

WAYLON OPENED HIS EYES, reorienting himself to the ER room. Dim fluorescent lights. Hospital gown. Scratchy sheets. Thin blanket. IV in his hand. Too many machines.

He longed for the comfort of his own bed.

"Did you have a good nap?" Melanie yawned from the chair she was seated in at his bedside and took hold of his hand.

"Yeah, I did." Between sheer exhaustion and getting his head knocked around in the accident, he'd needed the shut-eye much more than he had realized. "How long was I out?"

"You fell asleep about thirty minutes after they brought you back from getting the CT scan. So, that would be..." She glanced at the clock on the wall. "About four hours."

It was already past noon.

The truck that ran them off the road had fled the scene after they'd broken through the guardrail. The slide down the slope had been terrifying in the dark with no way to tell how far they'd had to fall.

Fortunately, it had only been a few hundred feet down the embankment when they'd slammed into the trunk of one of Colorado's venerable old ponderosa pines. It had taken a lot of time to get them out of the ravine, to fill out a police report and to have a battery of tests run on him. Melanie had whiplash but was otherwise okay.

So far, the police had nothing on the other driver or the exact make and model of the truck that had driven them off the road.

His GMC was now an old hunk of metal. Totaled in the accident that had nearly killed them both.

They were lucky to be alive.

"Is the cop they assigned still here?" He'd refused to leave her alone for a CT scan or to even sleep until the police had agreed to post an officer by the room, protecting Melanie.

"Yes. We have not one, but two. A second officer arrived a little bit after you fell asleep."

He was relieved the local authorities were taking the threat seriously. "Did I miss anything important while I was sleeping?"

"I updated Holden and JJ about the accident and asked

the two to keep each other in the loop. Also, I finally spoke to Emilio Vasquez. The investigator I used to work with in Denver."

"And? Is he okay?"

"He's fine." She nodded. "So is his family, but he's angry about the situation, the recent string of victims, what's happened to Kristin. They became friends during the Colter case." Lowering her head, she bit her lip. "We're all so worried about her. She's been missing for more than thirteen hours," she said, her voice choked with emotion.

The implication hung in the air between them. The odds of finding Kristin Loeb alive at this point were slim and plummeted further with each passing minute.

She looked up at him, her eyes glistening with tears. "This is all my fault. Once we found out what room Kristin was in, we should've changed ours to be as close to hers as possible. I should have texted her our room number. Set chairs out on the walkway and waited for her outside. There were so many things I should've done differently instead of allowing myself to get distracted with you."

The blow hit him hard and deep. He squeezed his eyes closed against the sudden jab of pain in his chest. Melanie regretted sleeping with him. Blamed herself for what had happened to Kristin.

Opening his eyes, he met hers. "This isn't your burden to carry. The fault is mine. More mine than yours. I've underestimated who we're up against at every turn. At the motel, the Sand Angelite house, on Route 287." Making mistakes wasn't like him. They were being outmaneuvered. Without a full understanding of the enemy, who was operating two steps ahead, they were blindly chasing their tails. "Don't blame yourself." He didn't want her to put that unbearable weight on her shoulders. "Blame me instead."

"I can't. It wouldn't be fair to you."

"Guilt and blame aren't going to solve anything. Those are the real distractions. That's what Colter wants."

Her gaze fell, like she was thinking. "You're right. That is precisely what he wants. He told me as much when I questioned him."

"Colter is determined to get under your skin. Don't let him. Kristin might still be alive. We have to believe that until we have a concrete reason not to." If Colter was going to kill her, or have someone else do it, he'd want Melanie to know she was dead. They had to treat this as a missing person case until her body was found. "You're alive. So is Vasquez. Let's not waste time beating ourselves up. Okay?"

She hesitated. "I'll try."

"What about Vasquez's family? Are they in protective custody or being watched?"

"He left his family behind in Florida with relatives for their safety and came back alone. Emilio is determined to investigate. Using his big gun, a hacker he's relied on from time to time. Orson. The guy has a genius-level IQ. Hacked into some government agency when he was only fourteen. Also, Stoltz and JJ are working the case together and are going to keep a close eye on Emilio, and make sure nothing happens to him. Since Emilio and I are both protected, JJ is going to use his time focusing on the case instead of playing watchdog at the FCTC. He plans to put pressure on Kurt Parrish and question the other men staying at the center, like I suggested. The Denver PD will have eyes on the front and back of the FCTC at night. JJ hopes that additional manpower will be approved to follow Colter during the day, too."

"Any idea what the holdup is?"

"JJ thought Kristin's kidnapping would ensure things were fast-tracked, and to some extent it was, regarding eyes on the FCTC, but his captain is reluctant to authorize more manpower."

"Why?" One convicted killer was free and people he had a vendetta against were turning up dead or kidnapped.

"All the evidence points to a copycat and Kurt Parrish is supplying an airtight alibi for Colter. JJ is going to try to go over his captain's head for approval."

Waylon winced. "That's not going to go over well."

"JJ is aware and willing to take the risk. Hopefully, they can get Parrish or one of the other men at the center to give them something. Stoltz submitted a request for Colter's list of visitors and copies of his mail to the supermax in Florence, and Emilio will be helping investigate. I'm sure we'll get something to go on."

"There's a lot for Vasquez to dive into. Any idea where he's going to begin?"

"Finding Kristin is his priority. We're hoping she's still alive." Melanie shoved her hair behind her ear. "I forwarded him my texts from her and he has the notebook that you got at Meacham's. He's going to get the detectives to check her home computer. Emilio said all her notes on her laptop should've synced automatically to the cloud. I hope there's something for him to go on. That it wasn't all in her notebooks."

"He'll find something." He tightened his fingers on hers, wishing they weren't stuck in a hospital when they should be investigating themselves. "Don't worry."

"I hope that's not just wishful thinking or you trying to make me feel better."

"Emilio must be excellent at his job because you chose him as your go-to investigator. Speaks volumes about him. And he's using a topnotch hacker. Emilio has skin in the game. You were attacked, Kristin was taken, and his name is on Colter's hit list. If there's something to go on, any lead, Emilio Vasquez will find it."

She took a deep breath. "You make a good point. I do tend to choose individuals who are not only adept but also relentless." She flashed him a smile that made his chest ache for an entirely different reason.

A question he had for her had been niggling at him since the doctor had examined her and deemed her okay aside from whiplash. "Earlier, between the tests, with the doctors and nurses coming in and out, it didn't seem the right time to ask." He'd had bloodwork, a neurological exam, cognitive testing and brain imaging. "The thing with Luna Tuttle, are we okay?"

Her brow furrowed. She shook her head and his heart sank.

"I'm sorry," he said. For falling for Tuttle's ploy and for asking about their status when she was worried about her friend Kristin.

But their relationship was important, too.

For nearly three years, he'd put his feelings and their situation on the back burner. If they couldn't face this together, after almost dying, then maybe they never would.

"I didn't mean to upset you," he added.

"Don't be sorry. I let Colter get into my head. I shouldn't have. All that matters is we survived."

That wasn't all that mattered. He wanted more than just to survive. "You matter, how you feel, what you think. In the motel room, when we argued, you thought we were doomed to fail and in the car, you said, *it figures*, like you expected me—"

She pressed her fingers to his lips, silencing him. "The doctor said you're supposed to rest."

Waiting, avoiding, stonewalling only squandered precious time. He was done with that. Waylon lowered her hand from his mouth. "What did you mean by 'it figures'?"

"It's just…" She glanced away from him, her expression turning inscrutable. "Nothing important. I shouldn't have said it."

Dealing with messy emotions wasn't her strength, and he could see she was bleeding, on the inside. A deep wound he needed to expose. "You don't say things you don't mean. I need you to tell me. Even if you think it'll hurt me."

Taking a breath, she rested a hand on his chest and looked at him. "Every person I've ever been close to, every guy I've dated, has let me down, disappointed me in some way. Even my parents. It's taught me that it's a mistake to depend on others, to need them."

"The guys you dated were probably jerks. Like Brent. Guys you chose because you never wanted to get close to them. Never wanted to love them. As for your parents, when you've talked to me about your years at boarding school, I could see it bothered you. The loneliness. What it was like being a minority there." Exeter, Harvard undergrad, Yale law school. How she'd felt different and struggled to fit in until she'd embraced who she was and decided to stand out. "It's like this sore spot for you with your parents. But they love you."

During their time together, she'd taken a few calls on speaker at her place or his. Her mother's voice had radiated warmth. Her dad, Frederick, always had supportive words, praised her, told her she was the brightest and could achieve anything. How they'd both uplifted her, encouraging her to be the best version of herself without tearing her down.

It was also clear that they had hardwired ambition into her and, along with that, came high standards she'd felt pressure to meet.

"I know they do." Looking unconvinced, Mel pulled on her trademark work smile that he'd learned was one hundred percent phony.

"They just don't show it the way you want. Every time they paid for school, bought you an expensive gift, that was them saying they love you. That they want to take care of you. They're not perfect. Neither am I. They make mistakes. So will I. So will you. But I want to be there for you. No matter what, I'll show up for you, big things, little things. When you need me most, I won't let you down. I promise."

Fresh tears sprang to her eyes. "I'm scared."

Melanie was a warrior with a chink in the armor. A wound of some kind. Before coming to Colorado with her, he'd figured it was heartbreak over a guy in her past. But now he realized she'd never invested enough emotionally to get her heart broken.

"Scared of what, darling?"

"That it won't work. *Us.* Our jobs, the conflict of interest. Our lifestyles, the long work hours. How to juggle a family and be there for children. I won't abandon mine, exiling them to boarding schools. I'm afraid that I'll disappoint you. Break your heart again. That you'll break mine and I won't know how to go on without you. Waylon, you almost died. What if you had?"

The long list of her worries made his head throb, but now he saw her clearly. She was sharing the part of herself that she kept hidden in darkness. This was progress.

During the fall over the side of the embankment, terror had had a chokehold on his heart. He hadn't been worried about his own safety. Only Melanie's.

His last thoughts before he'd blacked out had been about her; how much he loved her, how he regretted not fighting harder for her.

Tears fell from her eyes and rolled down her cheeks. "That's my greatest fear. Loving you, committing to you, sacrificing for you, only to lose you."

He tightened his grip on her hand. "You can't have a rainbow without a little rain."

Her brow crinkled. "Is that a lyric from a country song?"

Honestly, he didn't know. Maybe it was. Those tended to blur together in his mind. "What I'm trying to say is everything that came before us was the rain. I want to be your rainbow, M&M. I would sooner hurt myself than hurt you. I want to make you happy. I know how you need to be loved. That you need someone to show up for you. To be present in your life. To listen to you. To hold you. To be your soft place to fall. Your safety net." They both needed that. "Let me be your huckleberry."

"Waylon." She got up out of the chair and sat on the edge of the bed. Leaning close, she caressed his cheek. "You make it sound so simple. So beautiful."

That's what taking a leap of faith was—a simple, beautiful act of courage. And he believed Melanie had the guts to do this with him. For him.

"I'm asking you to love me," he said. "To trust me."

"I do love you." She took a shuddering breath. "I love you and I trust you. More than anyone else in the world."

He wiped away her tears, cupped her face in his hand and kissed her softly, tenderly, full of every emotion in his heart. "You have no idea how long I've waited to hear that."

Through a hiccupping sob, she smiled. "I wanted to tell you last year. After we first went dancing. Then I lost the nerve. Started thinking about all the reasons not to say it. But the biggest obstacle to telling you, was…well, you."

Not the explanation he'd expected. "How so?"

"If I told you how deeply I felt about you, that I loved you, Waylon, you never would have stopped fighting for us. You would've been even more determined."

He couldn't fault her there. "That's true." He kissed her again.

"Our jobs, the problem that the conflict poses for me professionally, is still a big issue."

"Don't worry about our jobs. We're going to work it out." He had yet to reach out to Rip Lockwood, the owner of Ironside Protection Services. They had plenty of offices, but he wasn't aware of any close to where they lived. Taking a position with IPS might require him to relocate or travel a lot. Going from a secret relationship to a long-distance one wouldn't be ideal. Maybe he'd have to do that for a while until a detective position opened in Cheyenne, a city within easy driving distance in the next county over. He was willing to go through any inconvenience if it meant they'd be together, out in the open. "You won't have to sacrifice."

"I don't want you to either."

They deserved a real chance at happiness together. He was willing to do whatever necessary to give that to them.

"You said you trusted me, so I'm going to hold you to it." He gave her a small grin, not wanting her to worry. "Everything is going to be okay. Believe me?"

She pressed her lips to his and his chest swelled with affection for her. "I believe you, Waylon Wright. Because a cowboy is only as good as his word." A smile spread across her face, brighter, warmer, sweeter than sunshine.

He made a vow then and there to coax those out of her as often as he could and leaned in for another kiss.

A throat cleared, drawing their attention to the doctor who had slipped inside the room around the curtain. "I don't mean to interrupt, but your test results came back. I'm happy to tell you that everything looks good. Considering what you've been through. You have a grade II concussion and should recover with no problems. I want you to get plenty of rest. Don't overexert yourself. For the first forty-eight hours, try to limit activities that require a lot of concentration. Light exercise and physical activity as tolerated thereafter. It's best to have someone stay with you and check on you for at least twenty-four hours to ensure that your symptoms aren't getting worse."

"I'll be with him," Melanie said.

"Good. Glad to hear that. Any questions for me?"

"When can we get out of here?" he quipped.

"I can start your discharge paperwork. Should take a couple of hours to get it processed. Sorry that we're not faster around here."

Seemed typical for an emergency room in his experience.

"I heard your vehicle was totaled and that you two are from

out of town," the doctor said. "Are you going to need a ride to the bus station?"

"We're covered," Waylon said. Before his CT scan, he had called his brother, Gunner. Told him what had happened and asked him to give them a lift home. "My brother will be here no later than three o'clock."

"The timing sounds perfect. I'll go get your paperwork finalized."

As the doctor left the room, pulling back the curtain, he glimpsed the uniformed arm of one of the officers stationed outside.

"Are you sure it isn't too inconvenient for your brother to give us a lift?" Melanie asked.

He was close with Gunner, with all his siblings. Except his sister. "Yeah, it's no problem. He wasn't doing anything at his ranch that couldn't wait a day. Besides, we haven't seen each other since New Year's." After Mel had dumped him, he'd gone to visit his family and ring in the new year with them. It had been good to see everyone, to catch up, but it hadn't eased his pain or his loneliness. "And once he learned we nearly died, he was willing to do somersaults through a hundred flaming hoops if I'd asked him to."

Melanie chuckled. "I can't wait to meet him."

This was new territory for them. Admitting their feelings. Taking a chance on a real relationship. Meeting relatives.

They could work through the logistics and politics of their jobs, through the juggling act of having a family. They could have everything they wanted. Be happy together.

Provided they lived long enough.

He had to stop Drake Colter and find whoever his accomplice was before he tried to kill Melanie again.

Chapter Fifteen

Melanie was grateful to be back at Waylon's house. Tucked in his bed.

Safe and sound.

Early morning light poked through the curtains. The sound of a pan clattering pulled her fully from sleep. She rolled over in the bed to find Waylon gone.

Last night, they'd made love. They'd tried to resist since he wasn't supposed to overexert himself. She'd decided for the sake of his health to take full control. They'd taken it slow, spent the time memorizing each other's bodies all over again, escaping fear and frustration, savoring a second chance at life. At love.

Goodness, she'd wanted him. That feeling. The burning, insatiable hunger that made her euphoric and enraptured and emotional all at the same time.

Throwing on one of his T-shirts, she padded to the kitchen. Her entire body ached, muscles she rarely used protesting with every step she took. Although she had been given a clean bill of health at the hospital, aside from the whiplash, which was also pronounced, the doctor had warned her that she might feel this way and it was entirely natural after the accident.

She found Waylon standing at the kitchen sink in his underwear, washing dishes. He had made coffee and breakfast. A pile of hot blueberry pancakes waited on the kitchen island.

"I'm supposed to be the one taking care of you." She plopped down on a stool.

The kitchen resembled the rest of the house; rustic, warm, comfortable. She loved the details like the dark wood beams on the ceiling that were the same color as the hardwood floors, the stone-textured backsplash with German smear that he'd installed himself behind the stove.

Her place looked like a model house from the pages of a magazine while his felt like a cozy home.

"Figured we could take care of each other." He poured coffee in a mug and set it down in front of her. "You went more than a day and a half with no rest. I don't know how you were able to stay up, watching over me in the hospital. I wanted you to sleep in this morning and to wake up to a hot breakfast."

His mention of the time had her glancing at the clock on the wall. A little after nine on Sunday morning. Kristin had been taken two days ago but not yet forty-eight hours. Last night, it hadn't been easy for Melanie to fall asleep. She'd been racked with worry and guilt.

No news, no new leads, had only made it worse.

The cold pit opened in her stomach once more, the fear that Kristin was dead, the fear that Colter was unstoppable. The fear of not having a future with Waylon.

Would they get to have one together?

Melanie smiled nervously, not wanting Waylon to pick up on her worries. She'd promised not to get bogged down with guilt and blame.

They had to catch Colter and his accomplice. All his victims deserved justice.

She'd focus on getting it for them.

Melanie put her feet on the pegs of the stool and rose, bending over the counter to give him a kiss. "You really are the sweetest. And a good cook, too." Much better than her.

"My mother raised seven of us, six boys. She made certain

we all knew how to cook, clean, sew and didn't subscribe to notions of household chores being delegated based on sex. Plenty of times one of us boys were stuck in the kitchen or doing laundry while my sister worked the ranch."

"I'm happy to hear about the equality in the Wright household and plan to take full advantage of your cooking skills." Melanie gave him another kiss before grabbing her purse and sitting back down. Two messages had come in while she was sleeping. She scrolled through both.

JJ: ADX Florence info in. See emails. Loads to process. Wright cc'd.

Darcy: Let me know if you need me to come in to work today. Happy to help. Already cleared my schedule since you were out Friday.

Darcy really was the best, anticipating that Melanie might need her.

"Were there any updates while I was asleep? JJ mentioned emails from the prison." She figured it would be quicker to ask him.

"As a matter of fact, I was going to tell you about that." He gestured with his head toward the hall and left the kitchen.

Shoving her phone back in her purse, she swiveled on her stool, hopped off and followed him down the hallway, past the bedrooms and bathroom. In the front of the house, his living room and dining room were one large open space only separated by the walkway running between them.

"The visitor list and copies of Colter's mail came in. I spent the morning downloading and printing the emails." He waved his hand at the dining room table long enough to comfortably seat eight.

A printer sat beside three stacks of printed visitor logs and copied correspondence covering three years.

"How long have you been awake?"

"Awhile."

"Printing all this must've taken an hour, give or take."

"Give or take. I was lucky I had enough copy paper. Good thing I buy it by the case instead of the ream." He tapped the box on the floor with his foot. "I volunteered us to go through everything. According to Stoltz, Kurt Parrish is definitely afraid and hiding something. They're going to interview his friends and family, and Vasquez will have access to Kristin's computer today. Also, there are finally officers assigned to watch Drake Colter around the clock. If he leaves the FCTC, there'll be eyes on him."

"I call that progress." She turned back to the overwhelming stacks of paper on the dining room table.

"I propose we get started after we eat."

"You'll get no argument from me."

He slung an arm over her shoulder and they traipsed back toward the kitchen.

"That stack is going to take all day to sort through, analyze, and connect the dots on our own." Maybe longer. "How do you feel about me asking Darcy to come over and help? She's willing to work today and she's the best researcher in the office."

"I don't mind. I'll just have to do my best to keep my hands off you while she's around. The last thing I want is to complicate things for you by having someone in your office think that there's more to you staying here besides me trying to protect you."

"She already knows I was attacked at the office. Not as though I could hide it from her with the shattered door and crime scene tape. Also, she's aware that you're the one protecting me and drove me to Colorado. I don't think it'll be a problem."

Provided they didn't slip up in front of her.

The idea of their relationship no longer being a secret was welcomed. The specifics on how that would happen were still unknown to her, but she trusted Waylon to come up with a solution they could both accept.

"Eat first." Waylon shoved the stack of pancakes closer to her. "Then reach out to Darcy." He slid her purse down the kitchen island to the other side of him. "Boyfriend's orders."

She smiled at him. "Boyfriend" was too small a word for what Waylon was to her. Significant other. Partner. Her person. Stronger terms. Better suited to what he meant to her.

The yummy smell of the breakfast made her stomach grumble with hunger. She'd skipped dinner last night, unable to eat, anxious over Kristin. The more time that passed, the bleaker the outlook.

Her hope of them finding Kristin alive was waning, but she refused to give up until she had no other choice.

Another grumble from her stomach. Starving herself wasn't going to help.

She stabbed a couple of pancakes with a fork and put them on her plate. "Tell your mother I appreciate her modern parenting style."

His brother, Gunner, had been so much like him in personality and looks. Not quite as broad or tall. In football terms, if Waylon was the size of a tight end, then Gunner was built more like a quarterback. Handsome, too, in that rugged Wright way. Super polite to the point that he had called Melanie "ma'am" so many times it grated on her nerves until she had insisted that he call her by her first name.

Not only had he given them a ride back to Wayward Bluffs, he'd also coordinated with his other siblings and arranged to have a loaner car waiting at the house.

An old SUV. Beat up but dependable.

She respected their frugality of driving a vehicle as long as possible rather than always chasing the newest model. That admirable value had certainly crossed over into other areas of Waylon's life.

Once he committed to something or someone, he stayed committed.

"Tell her yourself," he said, sitting beside her. "Gunner pulled me to the side and told me she wants to come down sometime soon. Stay a night or two. Meet you."

"Meet me?" She grabbed the syrup and poured it on her pancakes. "Why?"

"Well, I may have talked about you when I visited at New Year's. She could tell I wasn't over you. Then Gunner told her that I had been in the accident with *my Melanie*."

"Hmm." She shoved a forkful of food into her mouth, stalling for time, and nearly melted at how good the pancakes tasted. Fluffy, moist, fresh blueberries bursting on her tongue. And he had heated the syrup.

"I can always tell my mom it's not a good time to visit," he said, "if you're not ready for that."

"It isn't a good time and I'll never be ready, so you may as well let her come. But our current problem may still be an issue for the foreseeable future." She prayed that wouldn't be the case. "Will it be safe for her to visit?"

"She wouldn't be alone. One or more of my brothers will be with her."

Melanie tensed. Not a mom visit, but a family visit.

"It'll be fine." Waylon put a hand on her lower back. "We'll do fajitas and serve strong margaritas."

She chuckled. "Is that going to be your beverage of choice to get me to loosen up?"

"You betcha. That or wine. Either seems effective."

A cell phone rang.

Waylon grabbed her purse from the counter and took the phone out. "It's your boss's wife. Mrs. Weisman."

"I wonder why she's calling." They were scheduled to have brunch in a couple of weeks. Maybe it was to cancel. Gloria was big on etiquette and didn't leave such notifications for the last minute if she could help it. Melanie took the phone from him and answered. "Hello?"

"Hi, Melanie, it's me, Gloria." Her tone was restrained, not as jubilant as usual. "I hate to disturb you so early on a Sunday morning."

It was after nine. Not early at all for her. "How are you? How's Gordon?" Her boss had been out of the office unexpectedly. "Darcy told me that he's feeling under the weather."

"Do you have a minute?" Something in Gloria's voice made Melanie stiffen with concern.

"For you, I have more than a minute. What can I do for you?"

"It's Gordon. He's going to be in the hospital a few more days."

"The hospital?" Melanie dropped her fork on the plate. "I didn't realize it was something serious." She'd been under the impression he'd had a cold or the flu.

"Yes, unfortunately, it is," Gloria said gravely. "Once he's released from the hospital, we've agreed that he's going to be at the house and won't be back to work."

Melanie reeled with surprise. "For how long?"

"Indefinitely."

Shock hit her like a physical blow. "Oh no." If Gordon wasn't planning to come back, then it would have been because of something awful. Her mind spun with the possibilities. None of them anything she could bring herself to say. "What's wrong with him?" she asked, hoping it wasn't what she imagined.

Waylon put a comforting hand on her shoulder and she was glad to have him there, beside her, her safety net.

My person.

"Cancer," Gloria said, her voice cracking with emotion.

"He's had it for a long time and didn't want anyone to know. He was in remission for a while, but it's come back. We've talked about it and it's time to tell people. When you get a chance, he'd like you to stop by the hospital and see him."

"Of course. I'll make it a priority." She glanced at Waylon. The concern in his eyes almost made her tear up. Going through Colter's mail and list of visitors could wait a couple of hours. Actually, it didn't have to wait, she could have Darcy get started while she went to see Gordon. "I can come by the hospital today, within the hour, if that's okay."

"He'd like that," Gloria said. "He's in Room 311. Thank you, Melanie. I know how busy you are. I appreciate you making the time."

Gordon was her boss, the best kind, who had put the office's full resources at her disposal without question. He gave her a great deal of leeway and she appreciated having him as a sounding board. But he and Gloria were also her friends. Her move to the Cowboy State had been a rushed one and difficult, under less-than-ideal circumstances. She'd been a fish out of water. They'd welcomed her into their home and lives when she'd known no one. Introduced her to people, helped her build bridges and make connections. Paved the way for her to succeed in town, professionally and personally, when they hadn't had to. She'd never experienced such generosity at any other office.

They were the closest thing she had to family outside of her parents.

"I'll always make time for you two," Melanie said. "See you soon."

As THEY STRODE into the hospital, Waylon ached to wrap his arm around Melanie, the way he would've done if they were out in the open with their relationship. But they still had some big things to work out before that could happen. So, he kept his hands at his sides.

Waylon hit the call button for the elevator. The doors opened right away, they got on and rode it up to the third floor.

Melanie had been quiet since the phone call from Mrs. Weisman. Waylon had learned Gordon had cancer, but after that, Mel had retreated. She tended to get that way when processing something important, whether it was a case or something that hit closer to home.

When she got quiet like this, pushing never worked. He decided to give her space until she was ready to talk. Then he'd be there, a shoulder to lean on, a patient ear to listen.

The elevator chimed and the doors opened. They made their way down the hall, passed the nurses' station to Room 311.

"Mel, my dear." Gordon held out his hand when they entered.

He looked frail, older than the last time Waylon had seen him in person. Maybe the knowledge of his condition colored his perception or the last couple of days, with his illness worsening, had taken a toll on him.

Removing her sunglasses, she took his hand and sat in the chair at his bedside.

Gordon already looked sickly but paled further. "What happened to your face?" he asked, sounding aghast.

Melanie grimaced as she reached for her cheek.

She'd taken the time to put on a little makeup, to mask the severity of her bruises, but she'd kept the application light, not bothering to try to hide them entirely since the marks seemed determined to poke through.

"I don't want to trouble you with the specifics," she said. "You have enough to worry about."

The office probably hadn't told him because he'd been unreachable in the hospital, no doubt with his wife as the gatekeeper of communication to keep his stress low.

"At least tell me if that's the reason Detective Wright is with you."

"It is," Waylon said. "Circumstances require ADA Merritt to have police protection."

Gordon's brow creased with worry. "What happened? Are you all right?"

"I'm okay. Thanks to Detective Wright." She pulled on a smile. "Where's Gloria?"

"Since you were coming to the hospital, I told her to take a break. To go home. Eat a proper meal. Take a nap in our bed instead of in one of these uncomfortable chairs."

That was love. The only time Melanie hadn't been with Waylon in the hospital was when he'd had to be taken for his CT scan, but he had ensured that an officer had stayed with her.

The Weismans had been together a long time. Thirty-five or forty devoted years. They were the gold standard of marriage in town.

"I wish you had told me," Melanie said. "That you were sick."

"Once people find out, they treat you differently. I wanted to keep it quiet until…" He took a deep breath. "Until I couldn't any longer and, so, here we are."

"How much time do you have?" She shook her head, like she'd caught herself, hearing the words. "I'm sorry. Is it rude to ask?"

He smiled. "That's what I love about you. Your honesty. The lack of pretense with you."

That was also one of the things Waylon loved about her as well. "I'm going to step out in the hall," he said. "Give you two some privacy."

She glanced back at him over her shoulder. "Thanks."

"I won't go far."

Mel smiled. "I know you won't."

Waylon left the room and leaned against the wall near the threshold of the open door.

"I might have a couple of years left," Gordon said. "If I'm lucky. Time that I want to spend with Gloria. Not in the office, hastening my demise with work."

"I don't know how we're going to manage without you," Melanie said.

"You don't need me." Gordon gave a light chuckle. "You're going to do great as the acting DA."

"Me?" The surprise in her voice was genuine.

For years, she'd wanted that promotion, but Waylon was certain that she didn't want it like this.

"It was always going to be you, Melanie. I didn't hire you to be the assistant district attorney. I hired you with the intention of you replacing me."

Waylon was thunderstruck by his endorsement, his confidence in her. Not that he should've been. Mel was extraordinary.

"I-I had no idea," she said, sounding as astonished as he felt.

"I wouldn't have lasted as long as I did without you taking on so much work. So many tough cases. Without complaint. You're not simply a rising star. You're an unstoppable rocket ship. You're going to go far. I could even see you as the state attorney general someday," Gordon said, taking Waylon's breath away.

State attorney general.

A huge job.

A huge deal.

Melanie had only ever talked about making DA, but for a person like her, someone so driven, once she achieved one goal, a new one would have to replace it.

In some circles he was familiar with, it was a shameful thing for a woman to have too much ambition. Waylon had heard both men and women speak on it. Antiquated, old-school thinking, in his opinion.

He wasn't sexist, but he had been guilty of assuming that Mel was a highly competitive and determined female willing to step over anybody who got in her way. That she might have burned bridges in Denver doing so.

The truth was the Brents of the world had taken advantage of her while she'd been busy building bridges. She'd had to work twice as hard to get to where she was today.

Waylon admired her for not giving up, not settling for less than she deserved. The level of her ambition shouldn't be the measure of her value or success or something she should ever be ashamed of having.

Melanie *was* a rocket ship and he wanted to help her blast through the stratosphere.

"That's so kind of you, Gordon," she said.

"Not kind. It's just the simple truth. You've got a bright future ahead of you. I've reached out to some folks, some powerful people in this great state. Called in all my favors on your behalf. Asked them to transfer that goodwill to you. To help you rise. To ensure your success. Even the best rocket ship needs fuel, propulsion, and an excellent guidance system. Great things are in store for you. I've been assured."

Waylon wished he could've seen Melanie's face. She was going to get everything she'd ever wanted.

"I don't mean to sound ungrateful," she said, "but why would you do such a thing for me?"

"Gloria and I never had children. We weren't able to conceive, and I didn't want to adopt. Shortsighted on my part, looking back on everything. I regret denying her the opportunity to be a mother. Since you came into our lives, you've been like a daughter to us. I don't need those favors anymore. Let me do this for you."

"Thank you. Mind if I hug you?"

"Bring it in."

Waylon peeked around into the room. Melanie leaned over and hugged Gordon.

"I don't know what to say."

"Say, you'll still call Gloria after I'm gone," Gordon said, patting her back "and have lunch with her on occasion."

As Melanie sat back down, Waylon drew back out of sight.

"It would be my pleasure," Mel said. "You know how much I love Gloria."

"There. Nothing else needs to be said on that matter. Now, you're going to tell me exactly what happened to your face and why you need police protection."

Waylon strode down the hall toward the elevator. Once certain there was no danger of him being overheard while keeping an eye on anyone going in or out of Gordon's room, he pulled out his phone and the business card from his wallet.

Hard to believe that Rip Lockwood, the one-time leader of the Iron Warriors Motorcycle Club, was an illustrious business owner who had built a small empire in security and protection services. The last he'd heard about Lockwood, from Melanie unofficially, was that he had helped bring down a notorious bad guy in town they had all been after for years.

The achievement had come at a great personal cost. Lockwood and a former sheriff's deputy he'd ended up marrying had gone into hiding from a drug cartel. The very same cartel that Waylon had helped the Powells deal with.

Waylon dialed the private number on the back of the card. The phone rang three times and he worried that it would go to voicemail.

His phone vibrated. A text came through, flashing on the top of his screen.

Holden: Kristin Loeb's body was found. Call me for details.

A thread of ice slithered through Waylon's gut and twisted. He was just about to hang up and call the chief deputy.

But, finally, on the sixth ring, someone picked up. "This is Rip Lockwood."

"Hello." His mind blanked. It took him a beat to gather his thoughts. "This is Detective Waylon Wright." He considered asking Lockwood if they could schedule a chat for a later time. But he had no idea when that would be, whether they'd get another break in the storm. Maybe it was better to take a few minutes to get his questions answered while Melanie finished her visit with Gordon. "Chance Reyes gave me your number. He told me that you might have a position available for me in Ironside Protection Services."

"First, let me thank you for going to war against the Sandoval Cartel. My family and I no longer have to keep a low profile in no small part because of you."

"Lives were at stake. Action needed to be taken. Without delay. I took it. Simple as that." The situation had been more complicated, but his explanation didn't need to be. He'd only done what was right. Necessary.

"Chance told me I was going to like you," Lockwood said. "He was right. I understand we have something in common."

News to him. Waylon didn't have any earthly idea what he could have in common with a former motorcycle club president. "Oh really. What's that?"

"Chance did a deep dive into you and gave me a very detailed dossier."

Another news flash. Waylon felt at a disadvantage.

"We're both veterans with a unique skill set," Lockwood said. "I was a Marine Raider."

"Army ranger," Waylon said, a reflex and unnecessary since this guy already knew everything about him.

The interesting part was not only had they served their

country, but they had done so in Special Operations. They were both force multipliers. Deadly weapons.

"You were highly decorated," Lockwood said.

"The military likes giving out medals."

"True, but you also received plenty of commendations as a detective as well. Those can be rare on the force."

"The goal was never about recognition but rather seeking to make a real difference in the world." In the fight against evil and for those who couldn't fight for themselves.

His thoughts veered back to Kristin Loeb. To the devastation that was about to hit Melanie.

To the monster named Drake Colter.

His gut burned with the need for justice.

"You're modest, too," Lockwood said.

Waylon's phone vibrated again. A text from Stoltz. Holden must've updated the Denver PD.

"Um, I don't mean to be rude," Waylon said, "and I know I called you, but there's a case I'm working on and I just received some information that requires my attention. Can we do this another time?"

"It's taken you six months to dial my number. Now that I've got you on the line, I don't want to let this opportunity pass. Give me two minutes. Hear out the proposition I have for you. Then you can take as much time as you want to think it over or reach out again at your convenience with any follow-up questions. What do you say?"

Waylon stared down the hall at Gordon's room. How was he going to break the news to Melanie?

The thought made his heart sink.

Everything good—their decision to commit to a real relationship, the door opening to her professional dreams—was tied up with the bad—Gordon's illness, the latest SAK murders, Kristin Loeb's body being found.

This wasn't just a simple storm to weather. It was a tsunami. One catastrophic wave after another, all triggered by a major earthquake.

Melanie was taking a breather, a moment to connect with Gordon.

Waylon had to believe they'd have a future together and needed to plan for it during this brief lull between the waves. He could give Lockwood two minutes. "I'm listening."

Chapter Sixteen

Emptiness yawned through Melanie. She wrung her hands in the passenger's seat of Waylon's loaner vehicle. A tense silence filled the SUV on their way to the crime scene.

Ice cold. Shut it down.

Be ice cold.

She repeated the mantra over and over, needing the emotional distance between herself and what she was about to face.

The sand dune came into view, and Melanie's pulse picked up. Three, *four* emergency vehicles, plus a KLBR news van, were parked off to the side of the road near mile marker 15. No proper lot to be seen.

This wasn't like any of the other sand dunes SAK had used, which had been state parks, complete with a visitor's center.

Then again, none of those had been in the wilds of Wyoming. Melanie hadn't even realized the Cowboy State had sand dunes. Much less within a forty-five-minute drive of where she lived. As close to leaving the victim in her backyard as he could get.

She tamped down the hot rush of anger. The sharp pang of guilt.

Be ice cold. Ice. Cold.

"The sand dunes out here, do they only cover a small area?" she asked, her voice having a tinny sound that grated on her ears. "Is that why there's no parking lot?"

"The Red Desert is massive. The largest desert unfenced

landscape in the lower forty-eight with over half a million acres of contiguous wild country that spans five states."

The emptiness inside her spread. "That's a staggering size." The number of acres he'd spouted off rattled in her brain. "I had no idea."

"But I did. I just didn't think that homicidal monster would follow us back up here to leave her body. It should've occurred to me after the accident."

Bad enough she was beating herself up, she didn't want Waylon torturing himself, too. "You mean the accident that almost killed us and left you with a concussion. Even if it had occurred to you, little good it would've done. This is no state park where entrances can be monitored and patrolled. Out here, he has free rein." A chill skittered down her spine and she scrubbed her hands on her thighs.

Waylon placed one of his large warm palms on top of hers. "We can take as long as you need. There's no hurry to get to the crime scene."

At least he hadn't once asked the predictable *Are you all right?* She'd been prepared for it, but it hadn't come.

I'm alive. Kristin isn't. She was not all right. Would never again be all right until she brought her killer to justice. She guessed Waylon suspected as much.

"Waiting any longer won't make this any easier," she said. "We should go."

Her phone chimed with a text.

Darcy: Hank came over to help go through the documents since you're busy with other things. He also brought lunch, sandwiches, for everyone. Hope that's okay.

Busy with other things.

Such a simple phrase for one of the hardest things in her life that she was about to do.

"What's up?" Waylon asked.

"Darcy's boyfriend is also at the house, helping to comb through the documents." She started typing a reply. "He's a nice kid." Hank was Darcy's age, only seven years younger than Melanie, but they both had a youthful, starry-eyed quality. "A paralegal, too, with a firm in Bison Ridge."

Mel: No problem. Thanks.

"If he's anything like Darcy, the way she showed up armed with a variety of highlighters and different-colored sticky notes, then I'm all for the extra assistance today," Waylon said. "It's been one thing after another."

"Kristin is dead. This isn't another thing to do or manage."

He stilled. "I know. She was smart and dedicated. Warm and funny. And she was your friend." He took her hand and held it.

Melanie glanced at him. Her throat tightened at the look of love on his face. Tears stung her eyes.

She pulled her hand free before her emotions started spilling out and she unraveled into a sobbing mess. "I'm ready."

Waylon grabbed his windbreaker that had LPD printed across the back in bright yellow. He opened the door and a warm gust of air washed over them. They climbed out. She walked around to him while he pulled the jacket on over his T-shirt. Not that he needed the windbreaker.

Even at a glance, she could see they knew everyone out there. In addition to the sheriff's department, there was also a Laramie PD detective. Brian Bradshaw.

Melanie did her best to appear unaffected, in control, which worked until she hit the sand. Trudging through the uneven, shifting terrain tested her composure, threatening to break the dam holding back raw emotion.

Erica Egan, KLBR reporter and unofficial town nuisance,

spotted them and descended like a vulture ready to pick their bones clean of any tidbits of information.

A bubble of panic rose in Melanie's chest.

Waylon guided her past the reporter, positioning himself between her and the camera.

"ADA Merritt, is it true that you were close friends with the victim, Kristin Loeb?" Egan asked, maneuvering to the opposite side.

Melanie lowered her head, tilting it away from the news camera trained on them. "No comment."

Raising his hand at the camera, Waylon cut across in front of her, blocking them from getting a clear shot of her.

The relentless reporter refused to give up. "I was told that you provoked this latest murder because you don't know when to accept defeat," Egan said, and Melanie tripped, nearly face-planting in the sand, but Waylon caught her arm, keeping her from falling. "Would you care to comment on that?" She thrust the mic toward them.

"No," Waylon barked the single word.

They crossed the perimeter the sheriff's department had established. Two deputies prevented Egan and her camera-person from following them.

"Where does she get that kind of stuff from?" Melanie asked Waylon.

"Who knows? She may work for KLBR, but Egan is nothing more than a tabloid journalist."

Melanie was inclined to agree. Egan was drawn to sensationalized stories and controversial subject matter, always using a deplorable sound bite as a hook to draw viewers.

They approached the cluster of deputies.

Brian Bradshaw and Holden Powell spotted them and headed over to meet them.

"Glad you were assigned," Waylon said, shaking Brian's hand. "What in the hell is Egan doing here?"

"We couldn't stop her from coming," Brian said.

"Why not?" Melanie glanced over her shoulder at Erica Egan, who was making the cameraperson point the lens in their direction. "How did she even find out about the body or the location?"

Holden put his hands on his hips. "She's the one who informed us. An anonymous tip came in from the killer. Called the news station."

"The voice was digitally disguised," Brian said. "I've got the recording. I'll let you hear it, but I figured you'd want to see the body first."

They strode across the sand to the group of men milling near the body. A perimeter had been cordoned off. The only person inside the yellow-tape circle appeared to be the sheriff's deputy, who was also their current crime scene tech. He wore white Tyvek coveralls and a blue face mask and held a camera.

Kristin lay in the center of a sand angel. Her head tilted back, her face pale, blond hair fanned out like a halo, purple markings on her neck. Sand on her eyes. In her mouth.

Inches below her feet, a word was scrolled in the sand with stones.

Sinner.

The sight of Kristin and the rapid sound of the camera snapping pictures, click-click-click, made Melanie's stomach heave. Spinning around, she thought she might be sick and covered her mouth.

Waylon put a hand on her shoulder and squeezed.

"My best guess is that she's been dead for more than twenty-four hours. Maybe closer to thirty-six," the CSI said. "But so many different factors can severely impact the onset and timeline of rigor mortis. Temperature. Activity before death. Physical conditions where the body is found. The ME will be able to give a more definitive time."

"Why don't we step over here?" Holden suggested. "We'll play the recording the killer left at the news station."

They walked off to the side. Melanie kept her back to the crime scene. Part of her felt like a coward for not being able to look longer at Kristin. The other part was filled with rage.

Brian took out his phone. "You're going to need to brace yourself." He threw a cautious glance at Waylon and then back at her. "We can go back to your vehicle and let you sit down first."

Melanie shook her head and folded her arms across her abdomen. "We'll listen to it here." She'd rather do it standing. Less likelihood that she'd fall apart.

"Okay." Brian played it for them.

This statement is for Erica Egan. I am the Sand Angel Killer. I have chosen you, Ms. Egan, to spread my message. I want the world to know the truth. I want them to know my wrath, said the creepy, electronically altered voice. The cadence was sickeningly familiar. *To know that my most recent cleansing, of Kristin Loeb, the sinner, was provoked. ADA Melanie Merritt dragged her good friend into my crosshairs. She doesn't know when to accept defeat. Instead of the Denver DA and the sheriff giving a press conference, Merritt should have been the one standing behind the podium, on live television, begging for my forgiveness. She should have admitted that her judgment was impaired and biased while working at the Denver DA's office. That she made a heinous mistake, falsely charging and persecuting the wrong man for my crimes.*

The tone was whispery and raspy and cold and eerily insistent. *I'm willing to give her a chance to atone. She must show contrition, on the air, on her knees, begging me, by nine o'clock tonight, or I will claim another sinner before the sun rises and their blood, along with that of Kristin Loeb's, will be on her hands. Tick tock, Ms. Melanie Merritt.*

Melanie's chest constricted. Her heart started racing, palms sweating.

"You've got to be kidding me," Waylon said.

She squeezed her eyes shut, but saw the image of Kristin, dead, splayed out in the sand. Melanie had missed her at the motel by minutes. *Minutes.* The thought was agonizing.

If she hadn't gotten distracted, focused on Waylon, decompressing, making love to him, fighting with him, they would've been watching out for Kristin's arrival. What if they had spotted the tail on her? And what if they had put out an APB on him? What if they had caught him in the act, had gone up to the room to check on her sooner during the attack and intervened?

What if, what if, what if...

"Mel?"

She glanced up. Waylon was watching her closely. Again, he had the sense not to ask whether she was okay.

"Are you all right?" Holden stared at her. "Do you need a drink of water or to sit down?"

"What I need is to have Drake Colter back behind bars." She clenched her hands. "There's no limit to the depths of his depravity," she muttered under her breath.

A cold lump lodged in her throat and swelled. She felt like she was choking on it. Forcing herself to take a few deep breaths, she strained to stay steady on her feet.

Waylon watched her eyes, as if gauging her reaction.

She was used to seeing photos of crime scenes. Not being at them in person, forced to face the ugliness and senseless brutality up close and personal. For him, and the other two men, they had been to plenty of crime scenes and dealt with some horrid number of victims—the ones who had survived and the ones who hadn't been so lucky.

Waylon rubbed her arm, as though he understood her emotions pinged around like pinballs beneath the surface layer of ice she needed to get through this.

"Is it possible you got the wrong guy in Denver?" Brian asked. "Maybe the person who murdered Ms. Loeb is the real Sand Angel Killer."

Melanie opened her eyes and stared at him. "Drake Colter is a murderer. I'm one hundred percent positive. Not a doubt in my mind. The only thing that I might be wrong about is that he didn't do it alone."

Holden scratched his chin. "I take it, then, that you won't be making a statement of contrition tonight on the air."

"Down on her knees? Begging?" Waylon snapped. "There's no way that's ever going to happen. I won't let it."

Bristling, Melanie glared at him, annoyed that he knew what she was thinking. Except for the last bit. "I can speak for myself." She turned to the chief deputy. "Exactly what he said. I'm not making any such statement about impaired and biased judgment, that would only invite every criminal I prosecuted in the Denver office to have their attorney file an appeal on that basis." It would be a legal disaster. "I will never accept defeat. Or ask the forgiveness of a cruel, sadistic killer who gets off on taking human life."

Holden grimaced. "We've got ourselves a moral dilemma. I understand why you want to take a stand against this guy, but there'll be a consequence." He let that dangle for a moment. "Someone else will die. And that woman," Holden said, pointing to Egan, who was still filming them, "is going to tell the world that it's your fault. That you had a chance to save someone and chose not to. Can you live with the fact that by not doing what this sicko wants, someone else will pay for it?"

Bile rose in the back of Melanie's throat, making the tender flesh burn. Her thoughts whirled and gnawed at her. She didn't care if the world condemned her, but she didn't want anyone else to die because of her.

"Still time to think it through," Brian said. "Almost nine hours before you have to make a decision, either way, that you might regret."

Melanie glanced over her shoulder at Kristin's body again. The woman had been a good person. A whip-smart investigative journalist, passionate, caring, who hadn't deserved to die at the age of forty. At the hands of a monster. "I don't want anyone else's blood on my hands."

"No one's blood is on your hands," Waylon said, drawing her gaze. "This isn't your fault. You can't consider it. The criminals you prosecuted in Denver could walk free. Not only that, but you also have to think of your career. The long-term implications of making a statement like that."

Her career was important but preventing the death of another innocent person was far more important. "If I can save someone, then I have to, don't I?"

"You might not have any other choice," Holden said grimly.

"There's always a choice. Step aside," Waylon thundered, staring daggers at the chief deputy until Holden raised a hand in submission and walked away, Brian leaving alongside him. Then he looked back at her. "You don't have to do this." His voice lowered. "Mel, you can't negotiate with a terrorist. A known murderer. Listen to me. The way Drake Colter spoke about you haunts me. That sadistic killer blames you. Mostly you. And that's what this deadly game of cat and mouse that he's playing is all about. Hurting you *before* he kills you. That's the reason he had Luna Tuttle try to seduce me, because he picked up on our relationship. Now he wants to take away your career."

Waylon's jaw twitched with suppressed emotion. "Even if you do go on national television, begging some heartless animal for forgiveness that he doesn't deserve, there's no guarantee that he'll spare whatever victim he's chosen. And make no mistake about it, he has already chosen her. Trust me, you'll regret making a deal with this devil."

Waylon was right.

In her heart, she knew what he was saying to be true.

But she also couldn't live with the choice to do nothing, to not try. The consequence of another innocent person dying was too much for her to bear.

Chapter Seventeen

The summer rain shower only added to the heaviness Waylon and surely Melanie felt, making the air outside dense and muggy.

By the time they made it back to his house, the rain had stopped. Inside, Waylon couldn't believe the amount of work Darcy and her boyfriend had accomplished.

"Here's the log of people who visited Drake Colter over the three years he was incarcerated." Darcy handed them the sheets of paper she had stapled together. Her red hair was pulled into a high ponytail that swayed when she spoke in an animated way, like she'd had too much coffee. "Highlighted in pink are regular, routine visitors. There were six. I wrote their names on a bright pink sticky note."

Stephen Wolpert
Isaac Meacham
Luna Tuttle
Jovian Tuttle
Aimee Frazer
Nancy Colter

Waylon and Mel exchanged glances at the two names on the list they recognized. Isaac, cult leader supreme, was a no-brainer, and another name he knew too well.

Based on what had happened at the Sand Angelite house,

it shouldn't have surprised him that the Tuttles were also on the list. The skinny kid Stoltz had questioned in the kitchen turned out to be Luna's brother, Jovian.

"Any idea who Stephen Wolpert, Nancy Colter and Aimee Frazer are?" Melanie asked.

"Wolpert is his attorney. Nancy Colter is his mother. She stopped visiting last year because neuropathy in her feet became too much for her, according to her Facebook page. Aimee Frazer is a convicted stalker. Instead of being obsessed with celebrities, her preference is for felons."

"We know that Luna Tuttle is a Sand Angelite," Melanie said, "who idolizes Drake Colter. You wouldn't happen to know her relation to Jovian, would you?"

Waylon hadn't given her a full rundown of the who's who Sand Angelite list. "Jovian is her brother."

"Both their Facebook pages went dark about four years ago," Darcy said, "following the tragic death of their parents. The father died of a heart attack sometime after the mother was murdered." The redhead grimaced. "It's so sad."

"Murdered? What happened to the mother?" Waylon asked.

"You're never going to believe this, but the mom was one of the victims of the Sand Angel Killer."

Melanie rocked back on her heels, stiffening. "What was her name?"

Darcy leafed through her notes. "Celestia something."

A gasp escaped Melanie's lips. "Celestia de la Fuente." Her voice was low, her eyes haunted. "She went by her maiden name. Her husband declined to speak in court to influence the judge regarding sentencing."

"Yeah, that's right," Darcy said, looking at her notes. "His name was Rob Tuttle."

"Celestia had two kids, but I didn't know their names." Melanie appeared lost in thought. "I didn't make the Tuttle connection," she said, looking rattled.

Waylon folded his arms across his chest to keep from holding her or touching her in any way that would make it known they were romantically involved.

"Would you like me to make you a cup of tea?" Hank asked, like this was his house. Seated at the dining table in front of a pile of papers, the young man sported a trendy hairstyle cropped low at the back and on the sides, with the curly front hanging long across his eyebrows. He sipped from a mug that had come from one of the kitchen cabinets.

Waylon slid an annoyed look his way.

"I'm sorry. Darcy and I like to have tea while we work instead of coffee. I brought my own." Hank patted his messenger bag. "Chamomile. Lapsang souchong. Earl Grey. Spiced chai."

"No, thank you." Melanie dismissed the offer with a wave of her hand.

"Do you need a minute?" Waylon looked at her. "In the kitchen? Or outside?" Anywhere they could have a moment alone for him to comfort her.

"I'm fine."

That's what a warrior would say, but it was clear she wasn't fine.

Melanie took off her purse and set it on the table. "What else did you find?"

"For the rest of the visitor's list, if someone saw Drake Colter three times or more, but without any kind of routine, I highlighted them in blue," Darcy said. "And anyone who only paid a visit once or twice is marked in yellow. Green, I reserved for individuals who not only visited him but also sent him correspondence. They're written on the—"

"Green sticky note," Waylon said, completing her sentence.

With a bright smile, Darcy gave an enthusiastic nod, making the ponytail bob.

There were only three names on that list.

Stephen Wolpert
Nancy Colter
Owen Udall ➜ OHU

"What's with the arrow pointing to OHU?" Waylon asked.

Hank raked his curls from his eyes. "Only one person wrote to Drake Colter with any consistency."

"That's an understatement," Darcy said. "Try once a week for three years. I made the connection between the initials on the letters and the name listed in the visitor's log."

"OHU. Those are the initials in the return address and how every letter was signed." The young guy handed them each a sheet of paper. One letter was from OHU and the other from Drake Colter.

"What was the return address?" Waylon queried.

Hank grabbed another sheet from the table. "A PO box in Denver." He handed it to them. "Nothing overt stands out in any of the letters that I've read so far. Talk of how things are going in prison, what Drake had to eat. The other one mentions taking long walks, what OHU is watching on television. All innocuous stuff. But I think they may have been writing in code."

Waylon raised an eyebrow. "Why?"

Hank came around the table and pointed out something on each letter. "A passage in the Bible is referenced in every single letter. One hundred fifty-five from OHU and one hundred forty-two from Drake. At first, I thought it might be a way to share inspiration. You know, something hopeful. But then I started thinking about it. There's nothing religious about the tone. Nothing inspirational actually written. In fact, they both went out of their way to be as boring and under the radar as possible. Also take a look at the paragraphs, the way they're broken up. It's kind of odd. Like they wanted certain sentences, certain words, in a specific place."

Now that it had been pointed out, the oddity struck Waylon clear as day.

"He wasn't sure," Darcy said, "but once I took a look, I had to agree. They were probably using a code so they could communicate without being flagged by the prison when the letters were screened."

"Any idea what they were saying back and forth?" Melanie asked.

"No clue," Hank said, shaking his head. "We'd need an expert in code breaking. Even though we know they were using the Bible, the cipher can't be decoded without the key. Is it the numbers of the chapter and verse? Or something specific to the lines referenced in the Bible? It could take us weeks to figure out the true meaning of a single letter. Who knows how long it would take to decode almost three hundred of them?"

"Hopefully, Drake Colter and his accomplice will be behind bars in a matter of days," Waylon said. "Not weeks." He looked at Mel. Her gaze fell and she chewed on her lower lip. "What is it?"

"We don't have that kind of time." She glanced at the clock on the wall near the dining room table.

Two o'clock.

Her brow furrowed and she shoved her hair back behind her ears.

Waylon could practically read her mind. "You can't still be considering it," he said.

"I'm not considering it." But she gave him a baleful look. "I've already decided to do it."

Waylon set his jaw.

"Do what?" Darcy asked, staring at Mel.

"Nothing," Waylon said to the paralegal and turned to Melanie. "Please. Don't do this." The last thing he wanted was to start a debate with her that he wouldn't win. Especially when they didn't have any privacy.

"I have to," Melanie said, a determined look in her eyes. "Otherwise, I won't be able to live with myself."

Hank raised a tentative hand. "Excuse me. What are we talking about?"

Waylon groaned and, before Melanie could respond, her cell phone rang.

She unzipped her purse. As she removed her phone, the handbag tipped over on the table and the handle of his BUG slipped out.

Both Darcy and Hank noticed it.

Waylon tucked the handle back inside and zipped her purse closed.

"It's Emilio."

"Put it on speaker," Waylon said.

Melanie nodded and tapped the icon. "Hi. I've got you on speaker with Detective Wright and a couple of paralegals are with us."

"I'm here with Stoltz and Jimenez, but they're both on their phones. Melanie, I'm sorry to hear about Kristin."

"She was your friend, too. It's a blow for both of us."

"I have lots to update you on," Emilio said. "We were able to access Kristin's cloud. There weren't any recent notes from her. I guess they were in her notebooks."

Waylon swore under his breath and Melanie started chewing on her lower lip again.

"But she had her laptop, home computer and phone all synced. I was able to retrieve her browser history. The last thing she searched on the internet was Savio House. A nonprofit organization that helps to place foster children in temporary and permanent homes."

"That's what the text Kristin sent me was about."

"Yeah, I think so," Emilio said. "Savio autocorrects to Savior."

"What was the Savio connection that she found?" Waylon asked.

"Turns out that Isaac Meacham's father took in foster kids. Specifically, Drake Colter, Aimee Frazer and Owen Henry Udall. The last two visited Colter in prison. Not only that, but Isaac Meacham's father died under suspicious circumstances. One of the executive leaders at Savio, Vonda Van Nolan, told me that shortly before Bill Meacham's death, they received an anonymous tip that he was abusing the kids and subjecting them to brainwashing. Something to do with a new religious movement that incorporated the principles of Darwinism."

"That would explain a lot," Waylon said.

"Ms. Van Nolan also met with Kristin the night she was kidnapped. They talked about Udall at length. Going through the rest of Kristin's browser history, she must've pieced together that Udall attended law school at the University of Denver during the same time the DU student was killed. I think the last lead she was following was about him."

"Maybe she found him," Melanie said.

"That's what we're thinking. The last address Kristin used in Google Maps matches the current known address for Udall. My hacker, Orson, has been digging into Isaac Meacham's finances. Guess whose name Udall's apartment is rented under and who's been footing the bill for the past twelve years?"

"Isaac Meacham," Waylon and Melanie said in unison.

"Bingo. Meacham even paid for Udall's bachelor's degree in criminal justice and for law school, though Udall didn't finish. Hey, look, things are moving fast on our end now," Emilio said. "The detectives have enough for an arrest warrant for Colter."

"Based on what?" Waylon asked. "You guys must've turned up something concrete."

"Detective Jimenez got Kurt Parrish to break. One of the guys living at the Fair Chance Treatment Center admitted to seeing Colter sneaking out and Parrish helping him cover it up. Parrish completely fell apart when confronted with an eyewitness account. He claims the Sand Angelites kidnapped his girlfriend, who he's been dating for a month. Love at first sight and he's completely devoted to her. Parrish stated that they're holding her hostage and unless he does everything Colter wants, they've threatened to kill her."

Something about it scratched at Waylon's nerves, had his cop instinct pinging.

Melanie shook her head. "That doesn't sound like the Angelites. They're disturbing, but I've never known them to threaten anyone with bodily harm, especially not murder."

"Any validity to it?" Waylon asked. "Who's the girlfriend?"

"Luna Tuttle."

Waylon swallowed a grumble as Mel sighed.

The whole thing had been a setup from the beginning. Luna Tuttle must have cozied up to Kurt Parrish, got him to care about her, only to use that infatuation against him. "She's one of the Sand Angelites."

"Yeah, I'm aware. Stoltz told me that you interviewed her," Vasquez said, and Waylon thought, way to bury the lead. "Colter's airtight alibi is gone, he has a hit list tattooed on his arm and his Sand Angelite buddy appears to have been helping him the entire time. All that gave the detectives enough to get a warrant for Colter and Meacham, who's been aiding and abetting him."

"Meacham is a planner, a cult leader and the money guy." Waylon raked a hand through his hair. "He's been aiding and abetting, but he's not the one kidnapping and possibly killing people."

"Hang on a second. Detective Jimenez wants to talk to you."

"Hey, Melanie," Jimenez said, coming on the line.

"You're on speaker with my bodyguard and a couple of others."

"There's been a development." Jimenez's voice was grave. "I hate to be the one to tell you this." A pause on the other end.

"JJ? What's wrong?" Melanie asked.

Another beat of silence and Waylon's chest filled with dread. "Whatever it is, spit it out."

"The arrest warrant came in for Drake Colter. We reached out to the officers who were following him, but they lost him."

"What?" Rage leaked into Waylon's voice. "How in the hell did that happen?"

Mel's gaze was dark, ominous. She looked like a dam about to burst.

"Colter has supposedly been looking for a job. They lost him in the Park Meadows Shopping Mall. The place is pretty big."

Waylon clenched his hand. "How long has Colter been running around today with no one watching him?"

"Since nine thirty."

"How is that possible?" Melanie asked. "The mall doesn't open until ten."

"Mall entrances are open an hour before the mall stores do and walkers are welcome."

Waylon swore. "He could be anywhere by now. Why didn't the officers report in that they'd lost him?"

"They were embarrassed. Hoped they'd be able to find him before it was an issue.

"Listen, Colter knows he has to be back at the FCTC no later than ten tonight for check-in. He has no idea about the arrest warrant. We'll pick him up then."

"We think he might be working with a third person," Waylon said. "This Udall fellow. A man left a message for Melanie at the KLBR news station. Threatened to punish her for prosecuting the wrong man as the Sand Angel Killer. You need to find Udall and bring him in for questioning."

"Already working on it. Don't worry. This son of a gun is going down. Once we have him in custody, we'll let you know."

"Thanks," Waylon said.

Melanie disconnected. The worry on her face mirrored the same concern that had his pulse pounding.

"Are we safe here?" Hank asked.

"Yes." Waylon nodded. "Colter doesn't know where she is."

"But what about his other accomplice?" Melanie stared at him. "The one who left the message at KLBR. He might know I'm here."

"He's got his sights set on another victim. Someone else he plans to use to hurt you before he comes after you again."

"I've been thinking," Melanie said, "what if he targets someone I care about? Gloria Weisman." Her gaze shifted to the paralegal. "Darcy."

The young woman cringed. Her boyfriend hurried to wrap a protective arm around her.

If the killer's intent was to inflict the most pain, then those targets would be high on his list. "I'll text Holden now about Mrs. Weisman." With her husband in the hospital, she was alone and an easy unaware target. "Call her and make sure she's safe. Tell her to stay at the hospital until a deputy gets there and to notify security now."

As Melanie strode off to the side and made the call, he whipped out his phone and quickly fired off the message to Holden.

He received a reply in less than a minute that Mrs. Weisman would be protected.

Melanie hurriedly explained over the phone. "I'm sorry to endanger you, Gloria." A pause. "Thank you for understanding." She hung up.

"What about me?" Darcy asked, pressing her forehead against her boyfriend's shoulder.

Hank rubbed her back. "Do you want me to stay at your place, babe?"

"Why don't we ever go to your house?" The redhead looked up at him, her mouth in a slight pout. "Can't I stay with you?"

Her boyfriend tensed for a second then smiled. "Of course you can."

"Sure you don't mind?" Darcy sniffled.

"Positive."

"Are you armed?" Waylon asked him.

The guy shook his head. "I don't care for guns."

Waylon stepped toward him. "Do you know how to use one properly?"

"Yeah, I do."

"I can lend you one until this is resolved and Darcy isn't in any more danger." Waylon had plenty.

"Please." Darcy stared at the younger man with wide pleading eyes. "It'd make me feel better."

"Okay." Hank nodded. "Just temporarily."

"I'll get you one from my safe."

"No need. I can give him the one in my purse." Melanie reached for her handbag.

Hank raised a palm. "It can wait until we're ready to leave."

"Thank you so much," Darcy said.

"Well, I definitely need a cup of chamomile tea now. Does anyone else want one?" Hank looked around.

"Maybe I'll try the chamomile, also," Melanie said. "To settle my nerves."

"Make that three." Darcy kissed her boyfriend on the cheek and then the guy looked at Waylon expectantly.

"None for me, thanks, but since you already know where everything is…" Waylon gestured for him to go to the kitchen.

"Three chamomile teas coming up." Hank strode down the hall to the kitchen.

"What did Holden say?" Melanie asked.

"He's going to send a deputy to the hospital. Only one problem. They don't have the manpower to watch over her for more than a day or two with everything else going on."

"Hopefully, that's all she'll need. I'll reach out to Erica Egan about making a statement on air tonight, before nine, since she already knows why I need to."

Waylon glanced at Darcy, who sat at the table, her attention turned to the letters. "Are you sure I can't convince you not to do this?" he asked Mel.

"This is something I have to do."

Porcelain shattered in the kitchen. "Is everything all right?" Waylon asked.

Hank tore down the hall and into the dining room. "There was someone outside in the back. A man, I think. But I can't be sure because they were wearing a black helmet."

Waylon's pulse quickened. The location of the crime scene in the desert and the roads they had to take to reach it, made it easy for someone to watch the area from a distance. What if Colter's accomplice, the one who'd left the message at the news station, had been staking out the Red Desert crime scene? What if he had waited to see if Melanie would show up, only to follow her back to Waylon's house?

"Stay here." Waylon drew the service sidearm holstered on his hip. "Put the chain on the door, call 9-1-1 and then Holden." Without waiting for acknowledgment, he raced off along the hall.

In the kitchen, he rushed to the sink, made sure the window overlooking the back was locked, and peeked through the curtains, darting his gaze around. Grass and trees as far as he could see. No one lurking about. But if it was the same man who had attacked Mel, no telling where he could be by now. Hiding behind a tree. Or a shrub. Or looking to enter through a window.

Slipping the chain on the back door, he wished, for the

first time, that he didn't live in such a remote location and had neighbors close by who'd spot a prowler.

An obvious prowler dressed in all black, wearing a helmet, skulking around his property in broad daylight.

Something about that was off. Felt wrong. Still, best for him to check the rest of the windows in the house to be sure everything was secure. Then he'd have the others hunker down in the living room while he searched outside.

Spinning around, Waylon froze as his gaze fell to the bottom of his stove, snagging on a tiny, red-blinking light—one that shouldn't have been there under the kitchen range. Razor-sharp coldness zipped down his spine. Wires surrounded the LED light that started flashing faster in warning.

He'd seen enough improvised explosive devices in the army for his brain to register what he was staring at. A bomb had been planted.

Inside his house!

Melanie.

Waylon made it two steps when there was a hollow *whomp*.

Heat and debris slammed into him. The propulsive force of the blast lifted him off his feet, hurling him through the air. The back of his skull smacked something hard. Breath exploded from his lungs with an *oomph!*

Black spots danced in front of his eyes. Bile scored his throat. Pain lanced through his body. Heaviness pulled his eyes shut and darkness swallowed him.

Chapter Eighteen

An explosion came from the kitchen with a giant crack of fire and deafening sound, fragments of rubble spitting from the doorway. The punch of the concussion shook the house.

Her ears rang from the jarring noise. Smoke billowed from the hall.

Paralyzed with horror, Melanie was crouched, cell phone clutched in her hand, cringing in shock. Then realization set in. The blood drained from her face.

Waylon. He'd been in the kitchen when the detonation went off.

Was he injured? Alive?

"Waylon," she cried out, praying he would respond. No answer. "Waylon!"

She lunged toward the smoke, but a strong hand snatched her arm, holding her back.

Hank.

Metal glinted in the light. The gun from her purse was in his raised hand. He swung the weapon, hitting her across the face with it.

The blow sent her whirling around, her hand opening on reflex, dropping the phone and sending it clattering across the hardwood. She slammed into the dining room table. Her knees buckled. Reaching out to steady herself, she fumbled for something to latch onto, knocking her purse to the floor as she fell.

Darcy screamed.

Gut-wrenching pain mixed with blinding fear rattled Melanie to the core. She saw stars. Blinked through the agony in her head. Her vision blurred. Her stomach heaved.

"Shut up!" Hank yelled at Darcy, who was still screaming hysterically. "I told you to be quiet!"

"Oh my God! Babe, what are you doing?"

Hank pointed the gun at Darcy. "Sit down and be quiet."

"But we have to call for help."

Melanie's head cleared. She searched the floor, her gaze flying over her purse, her keys, to her phone. *There.* On the other side of the walkway, near the living room.

She had started texting Holden, before the explosion, but had never had a chance to hit Send. She prayed that a neighbor had heard the blast and called 9-1-1, but she couldn't rely on that. Couldn't wait for first responders who might not yet be on the way.

Climbing to her hands and knees, she prepared to make a dash for the cell phone.

"Help isn't coming." Hank kicked Melanie in the stomach, sending a nauseating bolt of pain through her abdomen.

Then he turned to the living room and shot her phone. The cell bounced from the floor, landing in scattered pieces.

Darcy screamed again, the shrill shriek at the top of her lungs.

Hank raised the gun at her and fired.

Silence.

A dark red spot bloomed on Darcy's stomach. Stunned or in shock, the young woman glanced down at the gunshot wound and looked back up at Hank. "Why?"

"Because this was always meant to happen. You were a means to an end. *Babe.*" He stalked toward Darcy. "Don't get me wrong. I enjoyed my time with you and you're great in the sack. If I thought Isaac had a chance at converting you into a believer, things might've worked out differently, but you're too loyal to that woman," he said, pointing the barrel at Melanie, "to see the truth about her. That she's a sinner."

Darcy clutched her bleeding abdomen. "Sinner?"

"Her transgression is the worst. Our number-one sin. She messed with the wrong pack of wolves."

Hank fired again—the sound making Melanie jump—pumping a second bullet into Darcy. The young woman collapsed. Hiccupping gasps of air came from her.

On a burst of panic, Melanie scrambled up from the floor.

Hank lunged, ramming her from behind with a foot to her back. She flew forward, her head smacking against the hardwood. Pain roared through her skull.

A weight crushed down on her, centered on her spine, and he yanked her head back by the hair. "Time for us to take a little ride."

If he took her to a second location, her chances of survival were nil. Here, in this house, she had some chance to fight, to stay alive.

Melanie screamed and flailed. She groped for her purse, for anything to use as a weapon. Her fingers closed around her keys.

For an instant, she considered trying to stab him with the car key, but he had a gun. He could blow a hole in her with a simple pull of the trigger. Just as he'd done to Darcy.

The AirTag.

There might not be a way to stop him from forcing her to leave the house, but if she took the key, maybe it'd help the authorities locate her.

Waylon.

Was he dead?

She would've given anything to run to the kitchen. To see if he was still breathing.

She had hope that he might be alive and injured, and clung to it.

"Come on." Hank pulled her up to her feet by her hair and

shoved her forward. "Walk. We'll be taking my vehicle and you'll be driving."

Melanie pretended to double over in pain and clutch her stomach as she slid the key into the pocket of her jeans.

Hank jammed the muzzle of the gun to the back of her head. "Don't make me tell you again. Move."

WAYLON STRUGGLED to open his eyes. An acrid ether odor filled his nostrils. A sharp burning sensation seared the back of his skull.

Swallowing the harsh rush of acid, he lifted his hand—the Glock still gripped tightly in his fingers—and tried to focus. Get his bearings.

A wave of nausea made his stomach roll and quake as he forced his way to his knees, gasped from the pain in the back of his head, and then got to his feet. His mind reeled.

Smoke and dust worked down into his lungs, making him cough. He glanced around. Fire. Rubble. His kitchen was in pieces.

Shards of shrapnel from the stove had stabbed his right thigh and pierced his abdomen. Both fragments were large enough for him to remove without tools but small enough not to have caused serious injury as long as they hadn't hit a femoral artery.

A wood beam fell from the ceiling, crashing onto what was left of his kitchen island. Dust clung to his clothing and face. His gaze fell over the wreckage of his kitchen, landing on what remained of his stove.

A bomb. In his house.

Had it been Hank? Darcy?

Or had they been working together?

"Mel!" He gagged at the smoke. Waving a hand in front of his face, he coughed.

Limping, he hurried from the kitchen, down the hall. He had his gun up at the ready. His pulse throbbed in his temples.

How long had he been knocked out?

Pressure welled in his chest behind his sternum. She had to be alive. She had to be okay. If anything happened to her…

"Melanie!"

His already pounding heart slammed into his ribs at the sight of Darcy on the floor. Blood. A lot of it. Melanie and Hank were nowhere to be seen, and the front door was wide open.

Darcy gasped for air and reached for him with a trembling hand covered in blood.

Holstering his gun, he raced back to the hallway bathroom. Grabbed the med kit and a towel. Hustled back to the young woman. Wincing through the pain as he knelt beside her, he pressed the towel to her wounds. "We've got to apply pressure."

Two gunshots. Centered close in her abdomen. One bullet had definitely hit her stomach. He suspected the second had struck her liver. The blood was nearly black.

She didn't have long to live.

"Cold." The word came out from her lips as a raspy whisper. "Numb." She coughed, spitting up dark red blood.

Not good signs. She was fading fast.

Even if an ambulance was on the way, they wouldn't be able to save her.

She reached out to him again and he took her hand in his, still keeping pressure on her wound.

"Darcy, do you have any idea where Hank might've taken Melanie?" *Hank.* Owen Henry Udall.

She shook her head. "No," she said like it hurt to speak, to breathe.

"Please, think." His gut tightened with panic. *Hang on, Darcy. Don't die.* "Do you know where he lives?"

A small nod. More blood sputtered from her mouth. "Followed. Him." She took a choppy breath. "Once." More blood sputtered from her mouth. "So c-c-cold."

"I know you're cold. I'm so sorry." He tightened his grip on her hand. This young woman had done nothing wrong other than falling for the wrong guy. One more innocent person whose life was cut short by evil. "Where did you follow Hank to? Where does he live?"

"Followed. To. Blossom…" Another ragged inhalation. A tear leaked from the corner of her eye and her last breath left her in a sigh as her head lolled to the side.

Waylon roared, angry, desperate, sickened at this senseless loss of life. He'd lowered his guard. Let the enemy inside his home. Gave that animal the chance to take what he loved most in the world.

"Blossom what?" he muttered to himself now that Darcy could no longer answer.

Street. Road. Drive. Way.

And where? Wayward Bluffs? Bison Ridge? Laramie?

What was the house number?

Molten fury flooded Waylon's system and he wanted to explode in vengeance.

But that wouldn't do anything to save Melanie. Not until he got his hands on Hank and used that rage to beat the life from him.

He whipped his phone out of his pocket. The cell shook in his hand.

Think, damn it. Think.

Isaac Meacham had paid for Udall's apartment for twelve years. Maybe he was still paying.

Waylon dialed Stoltz. When the detective answered, Waylon didn't wait for a greeting. "Melanie has been taken. By a man named Hank. I think it's Owen Henry Udall. It's the only explanation."

The detective swore.

"Is Emilio still with you?" Waylon asked.

"Yeah."

"Have him reach out to his hacker friend. See if Isaac Meacham is paying for a rented house or apartment anywhere in Wyoming." He spouted off the most likely towns. "Possibly on a street or road named Blossom. I need this. ASAP. We don't have a minute to spare." Every second counted. Melanie might not have much time.

"We're on it," Stoltz said.

He disconnected.

Climbing to his feet with a groan, he dialed Brian Bradshaw. His gaze fell to the cell phone that had been shot to pieces on his floor. He limped past it and over to one of the front windows. Pulled back the curtain. Looked outside.

Hank's SUV was gone. At least Waylon knew what vehicle they were in.

"Bradshaw here."

Waylon quickly explained what had happened, the explosion, Darcy's murder, and gave a physical description of the man who took Mel. "Put an APB out on him. Hank…" He realized he didn't know what fake surname the man was using. "I believe his real name is Owen Henry Udall. He's driving a late-model Chevy Tahoe. Black." Thank goodness he recalled the plate number and passed that along, too.

But that wasn't enough.

Waylon needed to find Melanie. Now. He couldn't even go after them, not knowing which way they'd gone on the road at the main intersection. East toward Bison Ridge? North, deeper into Wayward Bluffs? South toward Laramie?

Or someplace else entirely?

A string of curses flew from his lips and he pounded a fist on the window frame.

"We're going to find her," Brian said. "I'll have Holden send a deputy out to your place right now." They hung up.

Waylon stared at his cell, wishing it to ring with a call from Emilio.

Limping back over near Darcy, he grabbed the medical kit and sat at the table. He flipped it open. Dumped out the things he needed. Saline. Two types of gauze, the regular kind and QuikClot Combat to control bleeding fast.

Gritting his teeth through the pain, he pulled out the pieces of shrapnel from his thigh and abdomen. He flushed the wounds with saline. The burning flare of pain made him gasp. He dabbed at the injuries, checking that the sites were free of metal and debris. Quickly, he applied the hemostatic dressing then wrapped a bandage around his leg and torso. He popped a couple of painkillers into his mouth and swallowed them dry.

Waylon had been lucky. If he had been standing closer to the kitchen range or if the payload of the explosive had been larger, he'd be dead.

But that still left Mel alone with a killer.

He shoved the med kit away and glanced at what was left of her cell on the floor. Melanie didn't have her phone. No way to call for help. To let anyone know where she was.

But what if...what if she had her purse?

Pushing up from the dining room table, he looked around. Her handbag was on the floor.

His heart sank.

Then he remembered, the AirTag synced to his phone wasn't in the lining of her purse but on her keys.

Snatching the leather bag from the floor, he dumped out the contents. Wallet. Lipstick. Sunglasses.

No keys.

Hope was a fragile bubble in his chest, but he didn't dare

give it oxygen yet. On his phone, he swiped over to the Find My app icon and tapped, opening it.

Keys popped up as active. Two miles away. And moving. The app brought up directions on how to get to the AirTag.

He could track them.

Based on their current heading, it looked like they were on the way to Bison Ridge. That delicate bubble of hope ballooned.

Waylon was on his feet, hustling to his guest room without thinking about it. At the Barska biometric safe, he pressed his index finger to the fingerprint reader. The LED light blinked green, unlocking it. He swung the handle and opened the safe that stood less than a foot shorter than him.

For a second, he glanced at the black-velvet box on the top shelf next to his pistol rack. The diamond engagement ring inside had cost him three months of his salary. When he had planned to take their relationship to the next level, to him that meant a proposal on the beach. Asking Melanie to risk more had to come with the promise of more.

A lot more. Like a commitment for life.

One he still intended to make to Melanie.

Waylon grabbed the shotgun from the adjustable gun rack, slinging the strap on his shoulder, took two boxes of ammo, shells and 9mm bullets, and his bulletproof vest. He doublechecked that his knife was still in his boot.

Armed and ready to wage war in hell, if need be, he rushed out the front door and ran to his SUV.

Hold on, Melanie. I'm coming for you.

MELANIE SLID A terrified glance at Hank. He was staring at her. The gun was pointed at her side.

Poor Darcy.

And Waylon.

Were they alive? Both dead?

Was she next?

Her hands trembled on the steering wheel. "You said you don't like to use guns."

"Not my favorite weapon of choice. I prefer to use my hands. More personal."

"You don't have to do this Hank. Or should I call you Owen?"

"To my friends, I'm Hank. But you're not a friend. You," he said, poking her in the side with the barrel. "Are." Another forceful jab that had her cringing away from him. "Prey." Harder this time.

She winced from the pain. "Where are we going?"

They were driving down a rural road that was the fastest way to get to Bison Ridge from Wayward Bluffs. This route had dissuaded her from living out this far when she'd first moved to Wyoming. At night, with the lack of lampposts, the darkness had given the road an eerie feeling. Quiet. Isolated.

Like it was the perfect spot for aliens to land.

In the afternoon, it was still quiet and isolated, farmland stretching for miles on either side and not a house in sight.

The perfect spot for a serial killer's hideout.

"You have a date," Hank said in a jovial tone. "With destiny."

Was he taking her somewhere to kill her? Or to toy with her first?

"I don't believe in destiny." Everything she'd achieved, she'd worked for and earned. But she couldn't deny that the way she'd met Waylon, the timing of them both in the right place at the right time, the instant chemistry, had indeed seemed like fate. "It's an excuse to wait for things to happen instead of making them happen."

"I made this happen. You and me together in this car, on this road." He laughed. "Doesn't really matter what you believe. But your destiny is named Drake Colter. My brother, for all intents and purposes, was on the way up here from Colorado when I first came over to Detective Wright's house to lend a helping hand. He should be waiting for us at the house by now." A chime sounded. "Maybe that's him, wondering about the timing of the festivities." Hank pulled out his phone. His brow creased. His face twisted in anger. "Pull over and stop the car."

"Why?" Her mind spun with possible reasons. Something was wrong. A glitch of some sort in his plan. Whatever it was, he didn't like it.

He lifted the gun and pressed the muzzle to her temple. "Stop the car."

Jerking the wheel to the right, she veered off onto the muddy shoulder. She wished there had been a streetlight pole for her to crash the car into. Or another vehicle. A large tree near the side of the road. Any distraction, even a reckless one such as a deliberate collision, had to be seized if she was going to get out of this alive.

But there were no houses for her to run to, no pedestrians to flag down, no one to call the authorities for her. Unless she managed to wrestle the gun away from him, or knocked him out, she wouldn't make it far.

She slammed on the brakes. "What are we doing?"

"You think you're so clever. Don't you? But you're not." Raising his phone, he turned the screen to face her.

Melanie's heart nosedived to her toes. The small glimmer of hope she'd had turned into bitter ash on her tongue.

A time-sensitive alert had popped up on his iPhone. It read:

AirTag Found Moving With You
The location of this AirTag can be seen by the owner.

"Where is it?" he yelled.

"I don't know what you're talking about."

"You've got an AirTag on you." Hank swore, calling her a foul name. "Give it to me."

"Please." She raised a shaky hand. "I don't have one."

"Drake wants you whole and unspoiled so he can damage you himself. But if you don't give me that AirTag, I'm going to put a bullet in you. Somewhere painful that won't kill you." He redirected the aim of the gun lower. "I'll start with one knee and then move on to the next. Where is it?"

Beyond the pain of taking a bullet, it would take away her ability to run. A small window of opportunity might open where she'd need to be able to make a break for it. But she'd never escape if he shot her in the knee.

He pressed the muzzle to her kneecap and put his finger on the trigger.

Shaking, Melanie shoved her hand in her pocket and pulled out the AirTag.

Hank snatched the small device from her palm, rolled down the window and tossed it outside. "Drive."

Melanie stared out the window to where he'd thrown her one lifeline.

How would anyone be able to find her?

She pressed down on the accelerator. The tires spun for a few seconds and she hoped they were stuck in the mud.

"Give it more gas," Hank said, and she did as he ordered.

The engine revved, the tires spinning, spewing mud, and then they were free.

She cursed her luck as she pulled back onto the road.

No cars behind them or in front. They were in the middle of nowhere and she was trapped with the devil at gunpoint.

"Like I told you," Hank said. "Help isn't coming. There's no rescue in your future. Only your penitence before my brother kills you. That detective, your bodyguard, the one Drake thinks you're sleeping with, is dead. And so is my fake girlfriend, Darcy. When the authorities find you, it'll be in the desert. Where you belong. Laid to rest as a sand angel."

Chapter Nineteen

Stomping on the brake, Waylon brought the SUV to a screeching halt. He glanced at the Find My app on the phone. According to the GPS locator, Melanie should be right here.

But there was nothing and no one around. His heart skittered.

Maybe the accuracy of the position was off. He threw the vehicle into Park, his gut tightening.

Wearing his bulletproof vest, Glock drawn, he jumped out of the SUV and followed the arrow on the app off the road into the tall grass.

A horrible thought struck him. What if she was dead? Her body hidden behind a shrub or a tree or in the grass.

No, no. He shoved the grim, grisly idea away and tried to focus. A lot of time and planning, probably three years' worth, had gone into this diabolical scheme to insert someone close to Melanie and murder everyone on the hit list. Hank would want to leave her body in the desert, in a sand dune. Not off on the side of the road, rushed.

And then there was Drake Colter. Who was MIA. Could he be here in the local area? Had he lost his tail just to come here and kill Melanie himself?

Waylon trudged through the grass, swiping at the brush, and his gut tightened more because he found the AirTag attached to Melanie's key chain. He picked it up and stared at it—his only way to track her. Gone.

Heart in his throat, he curled his fingers into his palm, battling against the fear and desperation threatening to break him.

No. He refused to let evil win. Not on his watch. Not with his woman's life on the line. He wasn't going to lose her. Couldn't.

He turned back toward his vehicle and spotted something that might help.

Fresh tire tracks. Starting from the muddy shoulder at this very spot, heading back onto the road. It must've been theirs.

He could follow the muddy trail for a bit, until it ran out, but without more to go on, it wouldn't get him far.

His cell phone rang. "Wright here."

"This is Orson. Emilio's friend. I was told to call you directly to save time if I found something."

"Please tell me you did."

"Isaac Meacham is paying for a short-term lease on a house in Bison Ridge rented under the name of Hank Ludal. I've got an address on Blossom Trail."

Waylon ran to his vehicle as Orson gave him the exact house number. "Thank you."

"I'm letting the local authorities know that an officer is en route and requests backup as we speak. I've also given them your badge number for authentication."

Waylon threw the gear in Drive and sped off. "How are you able to do that?"

"Don't ask. You're welcome." The line went dead.

Flooring it down the road, he prayed he'd get to Melanie before any harm came to her. He'd made her a promise that when she needed him most, he'd be there for her.

A promise he had to keep come hell or high water.

HANK HIT A BUTTON on the visor and one door to the three-bay garage attached to a newly constructed house on Blossom Trail lifted.

The area was remote. The house sat on plenty of acres. No neighbors within shouting distance.

"Pull in," he said, waving the gun.

Melanie drove inside the garage and parked beside a plain white van. The same van that had been captured on her home security footage and that had been used in multiple crimes, including the abduction of Kristin. On the far end was a banged-up dark gray truck. Most likely the one he'd used to run them off the road.

"Drake is here waiting for you." Hank opened the center console and pulled out zip ties.

Oh, God, no. He was going to restrain her. How was she going to fight? Run?

Survive?

"Hands behind your back."

She shifted away in the car seat, putting her hands toward him. "Tell me, were you the one who found out about the legal precedent to get Colter released?"

"Sure did. A professor brought up the case in class. I didn't think there'd any way to get him freed. Then that convicted murderer in New York was released. Sweet loophole, huh?"

Nausea washed over her in waves.

Warm plastic wrapped around her wrists and he cinched the zip ties tight until they cut into her skin.

He got out, keeping the gun trained on her, walked around the vehicle and opened the door. "Get out."

She did.

After he closed the door, he nudged her forward with the gun. "Go on. Destiny has waited a long time for this moment."

Walking toward the door that led inside the house, she searched for a weapon. There were lots on and around the workbench. Shovels. A hammer. Four-by-fours. A drill. Screwdrivers.

None of which she could use with her hands restrained. Hank was practically right on top of her, watching her closely.

He opened the door and pushed her inside the house, into the kitchen.

A television was on somewhere deeper in the house. Sounded like a rerun episode of one of the *Real Housewives* playing.

Hank shoved her down into a chair. Then he zip-tied her wrists to one of the slats in the back of the wooden chair. Putting two fingers in his mouth, he gave a piercing whistle. "Drake! I've got a bushy-tailed, bright-eyed rabbit for you to slaughter."

The television turned off.

Silence. Followed by heavy, slow footsteps approaching.

Then singing. The lyrics to a nursery rhyme. "There Was An Old Lady Who Swallowed A Fly."

"Perhaps she'll die," Drake crooned as he waltzed into the kitchen, dancing. "But in your case, ADA Melanie Merritt, there's no question about it. Today will be your last."

A greasy ball of dread dropped into her stomach and churned.

"I hate to ruin this special moment you've dreamed of for so long," Hank said, "but the cops are on to us. They've issued arrest warrants for you and Isaac."

"Does he know?" Colter asked.

"By now, I'm sure he does. He's probably sitting in a holding cell. There's nothing we can do for him. At least he won't spend much time behind bars."

The sick joy in Drake Colter's eyes dimmed as he swore.

"This might be a good thing in disguise," Hank said.

"Oh really. How so? Our brother is going to be arrested."

"In jail, he can recruit full-time. Look at what he did with the Tuttles. Even after their mother was murdered, Isaac still turned those two into believers. All because the mother had been having an affair. Just think of how many hopeless, angry prisoners he can convert into loyal Sand Angelites. When he gets out, we'll have an army on our side. We'll be unstoppable. But first, we have to make it across the border into Canada once you're done with this one." Hank tipped his head at Melanie.

Drake's evil gaze swung back onto her. "This all could've been avoided if you had only listened when I told you that I was innocent."

"I think we have very different definitions of innocent."

"I didn't kill those women in Colorado several years ago. My brother over here is the real Sand Angel Killer."

Smiling, Hank put a hand over his heart, the other behind his back, and bowed. "Those were my victims. That's why I was so determined to get my brother out of jail and why you needed to be taught a lesson."

"But your DNA was found on two of the victims," she said to Colter. "You had to have been involved in their deaths." Not only was she curious, but she needed to buy herself as much time as possible. The only way to do that was to keep them talking. She didn't know if she could get out of this. Every minute she stalled gave her another minute of breathing. "You were with them on the day they died. Weren't you?"

"I picked them out," Drake said, "had a little fun with them and held them for safekeeping until Hank was ready to finish them off."

That made him an accomplice to murder. "What about the women murdered around Santa Fe found in the sand dunes?"

Drake shrugged. "Those bunnies were mine. I hunted them. Killed them."

"Then you're not innocent, you sick, twisted monster!"

"But you didn't catch me for that. I was arrested, prosecuted by you and convicted for murders I didn't commit."

Hank knelt in front of her. "I saw the fine work my older brother was doing in New Mexico. Our foster father had encouraged spirited competition before we killed him, and Drake became the new alpha of our family. I saw how I could improve on his work. Elevate it to an art form."

"The sand angel idea," Drake said, patting him on the back, "was very impressive. I wish I could've taken credit for it, but unfortunately, I couldn't. And being blamed for it, how you got my girlfriend to lie under oath, ticked me off."

"I'd never allow a witness to perjure themselves. Maybe she knew what you really were and decided to stop you."

"Maybe." Drake stepped closer to her. "But that act of defiance got Georgia killed."

"Did you do it? Were you the one who killed them?" ·

"Every single one of them." Colter pulled up his shirtsleeve and pointed to the list tattooed on his arm. "Babcock. Sweeney. That backstabbing ex-girlfriend. Nosy Loeb sniffing around where she didn't belong."

"I snatched them," Hank said. "Held them until Drake could sneak out of that Fair Chance Treatment Center."

"Except for Kristin." Drake grinned. "I took her and killed her in the motel room and then handed her body off to my brother," he said, and her stomach roiled as fresh guilt washed over Melanie. "I even came for you personally, ADA Merritt." His smile turned menacing. "First, I had to poison the chili at FCTC that made everyone sick. Get Hershel to go home early. I needed extra time for the trek to Laramie. Thanks to Hank, I knew exactly where the cameras in the parking garage would be and I almost had you, too. Could taste your fear. Your pain.

"I even followed you after you were done with the police. But leaving the sand angel on your doorstep had been a mistake. Intended to be my calling card for the cops, but that clued you in and scared you off from staying at your house. I tracked you to the detective's place with my headlights off. You two looked cozy, pretty familiar, with his arm around you, guiding you inside. I wasn't sure how we were going to get past him, but it was only a matter of finding the right unstoppable force to take care of that immovable object."

"The bomb was my idea." Hank took a half bow this time. "I just had to keep suggesting to Darcy to volunteer her time to help you. To offer to come over to make your life easier."

"Now that your detective is out of the way, my wait is over." A malevolent gleam sparked in Colter's eyes. "It's your turn to suffer and die."

Her heart punched into her throat. "Wait. Wait. Don't you want to see me on live television, admitting that I was wrong. Down on my knees, begging your forgiveness? You could record it, watch it again and again."

Colter frowned. "I was really looking forward to that. But once I realized the cops were following me, it complicated things. Easier to kill you sooner rather than later." He dug into his pocket and pulled out a plastic bag. "First, let's have some fun. Remember what I told you the wolf loves most about the hunt. The fear in the prey. Nothing brings that out more than giving the prey a preview of what it'll be like to die." Holding the bag open, he stepped toward her, ready to put the plastic over her head.

Terror gripped her. Melanie screamed and kicked Drake Colter in the knee and kept throwing the heel of her foot into flesh and bone, determined to fight until her last breath.

WAYLON CREPT AROUND the side of the house. The loaded shotgun was slung on his shoulder and his Glock was drawn, at the ready in a two-handed grip. He peeked into one of the garage windows. Hank's Tahoe was parked inside along with a white van and big gray truck.

This was definitely the correct house. He had to get this right. Had to control the scene and his entry. If he messed this up, then Melanie might die.

He couldn't let that happen.

He snuck around the house, hugging the walls and crouching low. The curtains were drawn. The house was a good size. Lots of rooms. She could be in any of them.

Gripping his gun more firmly, he crept up to the back window. The curtains were parted. But he didn't rush to take a look. Instead, he listened.

One man laughed—a gut-deep, creepy cackle.

Another shouted, "Woo-eee! Look at her thrashing like a fish out of water."

"That's what it's going to feel like when I choke the life out of you." The voice was Drake Colter's. "The only thing missing is my hands around your throat."

Adrenaline drop-loaded into Waylon's system as he snuck a peek inside the room.

Melanie restrained to a chair, struggling to get free. A plastic bag wrapped tightly over her head. She couldn't breathe.

Drake Colter and Hank stood around her, mocking her suffering, enjoying her pain.

Rage lit a fire in him and he knew precisely how to control the burn.

He needed to breach quickly. Had to get that bag off Melanie's head as soon as possible.

Inspecting the door, he didn't think he could bust it open with the swift thrust of his bootheel alone. He holstered the Glock. Aimed the shotgun at the lock at close range. Steadied his breathing. Directed the heat of the fire blazing inside him and pulled the trigger.

Boom!

Waylon kicked in the door with all the force he could muster in his good leg and swept inside. "Police! Get on the floor!"

Both men froze in temporary shock, their mouths open, their eyes wide.

"Facedown. Hands on the back of your heads," Waylon finished yelling the order.

Hank lunged for the gun on the kitchen counter. The Smith & Wesson.

The SOB was going to try to shoot him with his own weapon.

Pumping the shotgun, ejecting the empty shell and loading a new one, Waylon redirected the aim to the man standing closest. He opened fire, blasting a hole in Hank, sending his body flying across the kitchen.

Melanie was kicking, thrashing with her legs, wriggling her whole body, desperate for air.

As Waylon pumped the shotgun again, Drake Colter charged at him, howling like a rabid animal, and tackled him backward.

The shotgun went off.

Boom!

The blast hit the ceiling as they stumbled out of the house and hit the ground. On impact, pain radiated through Waylon and he lost his grip on the shotgun.

Swinging wild and hard, Drake Colter punched him in the face. Once. Twice. The blows kept coming.

Waylon took it. Didn't fight him. Used the heat of that white-hot anger to absorb the punches. To sublimate the pain. Focused through it. Reached for the holster on his hip. Curled his fingers around the handle of his Glock. Aimed precisely where he wanted the bullet to go.

He fired, putting a slug straight into Drake Colter's cold-blooded heart.

The dead man collapsed on top of him.

Waylon shoved him off over to the side.

Jumping to his feet, he groaned through the pain. He sprinted into the house and bolted to Melanie.

Waylon tore a hole in the bag, letting in precious air. Melanie raked in a desperate breath. He ripped the rest of the plastic from her face and around her throat.

Throwing a glance at Hank, he checked to make sure he

was dead. His lifeless body was slumped on the floor. Blood gushed from a wound in his chest. The Smith & Wesson had fallen from his hand.

Melanie was hyperventilating, shaking all over.

Reaching into his boot, he pulled out his knife and cut the zip ties from her wrists. She leaped out of the chair and into his arms.

Waylon hugged Melanie tight, never wanting to let her go. "Let's get you out of here. Away from this." The death. The terror.

"Thank God you came." She started crying, clinging to him, sobbing so hard, as if the only thing holding her together was his embrace. "I thought he might've killed you."

"You're not getting rid of me that easily."

She wept harder and chuckled, all mixed together in a tearful jumble.

Keeping his arms around her, he guided her out the back door, past Colter, around the house, to his SUV. Sirens wailed in the distance, drawing closer but still minutes from arriving.

He sat Melanie in the passenger's seat and caressed her face. "I've never been so scared in my life." He'd been terrified to lose her.

"I couldn't tell. You were so fast. So controlled. You were amazing."

"That was just training. What they don't prepare you for is this. Coming so close to losing the one person who means everything."

She threw her arms around his neck and hugged him again. "But you didn't lose me. And I didn't lose you. We're alive. Despite the odds. I think that means Hank or Owen Henry Udall was right about one thing."

He pulled back and looked into her beautiful eyes. "What's that?"

"Destiny. It's real. And you're mine."

Five days later...

Dusk settled over the Atlantic, but the temperature didn't drop with the sun. Melanie nestled up against Waylon on the two-person chaise longue the Saint Lucian resort had set up for them on the beach under a wide umbrella.

Listening to the waves break on shore and watching the sun set on the horizon, she was filled with gratitude to have this moment with him. "I'm sorry we didn't do this at Christmas."

He tucked her closer and rubbed her arm. "We weren't ready."

"Still, it shouldn't have taken both of us nearly dying for us to decide to be together and go on vacation. You know, when we get back, we're going to have to figure out how to handle things with our jobs."

"Already done."

She pulled away, leaned up on her forearm and stared at him. "What do you mean? What's done?"

"I quit."

Whipping off her sunglasses, Melanie's jaw unhinged. "But we were supposed to come up with a fair solution. I didn't want you to quit."

"Forget about fair. I didn't want you to compromise on your dreams. Why should you?"

"Because one of us had to and I didn't want it to be you." A life with Waylon was worth any sacrifice. She saw that now.

"There's no rule that states either of us had to lose something." He slid his shades down the bridge of his nose and looked at her. "Do you really want to get into this now? I was hoping we could wait until our candlelight dinner."

"I'd rather hear that you're unemployed and what the plan is without candlelight."

"Okay. First, I'm not unemployed. I accepted a position

with Ironside Protection Services. I spoke with the owner, Rip Lockwood."

Melanie was well acquainted with Rip and his wife, Ashley. Last she'd heard, they were expecting their first child. "Doing what?"

"Turns out that he has an informal office in our local area. Gigs that the Iron Warriors handle, mostly protection and security details. Anyway, with him gone, he was looking for someone to run the office. Not only to deal with the Iron Warriors, but also recruit, expand the scope of work into more investigative stuff. As a detective and veteran, he thought I'd be perfect, especially when it comes to liaising with the local authorities."

"Wow. So, you'd go from a one- or two-person show with the Laramie PD to being a boss."

"Team leader. Making double what I earn now. Plus recruitment bonuses. I'd only have to report to Rip, but would be given the leeway to run things as I see fit."

"That's..." She was at a loss for words. "Perfect."

"I thought so. That's why I accepted and quit."

Leaning close, she slid her leg between his thighs and ran her hand up his beautiful, hunky, bare chest. "We have to celebrate."

"I agree." He slid his palm along her thigh over her bikini cover-up. "I was thinking we should have a party."

She reeled back. "A party? With people?"

"Yeah. With our families. Maybe a couple of others like the Powells." He moved his hand from her leg, dipped into their beach tote bag, and took out a black-velvet box. "An engagement party."

Melanie's heart skipped a beat.

His eyes were warm and serious. The tender expression on his face made her legs so weak they might've given out on her if she were standing.

"I was going to do this at dinner." Looking nervous, he opened the box and took out a stunning pear-shaped diamond ring.

"Waylon." She sucked in a breath.

He took her hand, his fingers big and callused, and slid the ring on her finger. "I love you, M&M. More than anything in this world. I want to be there for you, no matter what life throws at us, now and forever. Will you do me the honor of marrying me, darling?"

"Oh my gosh!" she squealed, not realizing excitement would fill her to bursting at this moment. She wrapped her arms around him and squeezed him tightly. "I love you, too."

"Is that a *yes*?"

"Yes." Feeling a giant sigh of relief from him, she pulled back and smiled. "Yes, Waylon. I'll be your huckleberry."

* * * * *